ALSO BY

JEAN-CLAUDE IZZO

Total Chaos
Chourmo
Solea
The Lost Sailors

A SUN FOR
THE DYING

Jean-Claude Izzo

A SUN FOR
THE DYING

*Translated from the French
by Howard Curtis*

Europa
editions

Europa Editions
116 East 16th Street
New York, N.Y. 10003
www.europaeditions.com
info@europaeditions.com

Copyright © 1999 by Flammarion
First Publication 2008 by Europa Editions

Translation by Howard Curtis
Original Title: *Le soleil des mourants*
Translation copyright © 2008 by Europa Editions

This work has been published thanks to support from
the French Ministry of Culture – Centre National du Livre
Ouvrage publié avec le concours du Ministère
Français chargé de la Culture – Centre National du Livre

Library of Congress Cataloging in Publication Data is available
ISBN 978-1-933372-59-4

Izzo, Jean-Claude
A Sun for the Dying

Book design by Emanuele Ragnisco
www.mekkanografici.com

Prepress by Plan.ed – Rome

Printed in the United States of America

CONTENTS

PART TWO

AUTHOR'S NOTE

It would be wrong to claim that this novel is purely imaginary. I have simply taken certain aspects of real life to an extreme, giving names to, and inventing stories for, people we see every day on the street. People we can't even bear to look at. In other words, we can all recognize ourselves in these pages. The living and the dying.

To the wounded men,
and the women who survive them,
not always very easily, if truth be told.

For Catherine,
for this love

You must remember the color
of your wound in order
to warm it in the sun.

JULIET BERTO

PROLOGUE

Titi had the winter inside him. It seemed to him at that moment that the cold was even more intense in his body than on the street. Maybe that was why he'd stopped shivering, he thought. Because he was just one big block of ice, like the water in the gutters.

A lighted sign over the entrance to a drugstore showed the temperature, -16° Fahrenheit, and the time—a minute after eight in the evening. Sheltering as best he could in the doorway of an apartment building, Titi had watched the minutes pass, one by one, since 7:30. Then everything had become blurred because of the icy air. He'd realized that the mobile soup kitchen wouldn't be passing, that it was pointless to keep waiting for it. Every down-and-out knew the white van, knew its itinerary like the back of his hand: Place de la Nation, Place de la République, Place des Invalides, Porte d'Orléans. The fucking van never ever came through Place de l'Hôtel de Ville! But that was where he was, Place de l'Hôtel de Ville.

"Fuck!" he screamed at himself in his head. "You're losing it, Titi!" He looked at the lighted sign again, but everything was still blurred. "Hey, no point in screaming like that, you jerk!" he answered himself. "I know, I know . . ."

Yes, he was losing his marbles a little more every day. Rico had told him that, as soon as the cold weather started. Told him to go to hospital and get himself looked after. But Titi didn't want to go to any hospital.

"You're going to die," Rico had said.

"Yeah? So what? You go to the hospital, you're already dead. You go in, you come out feet first. Would you go? Would you?"

"You piss me off, Titi!"

"Fuck you!"

Since then, he'd stopped talking. Not just to Rico. To any-body. Or almost stopped. He couldn't handle talking anymore, anyway. He didn't have the strength.

In front of him, the lights turned red for the second time. "Fucking winter," he muttered to himself, just to summon up the courage to cross. He was scared his bones would break like stalactites. But he had to cross, to get to the metro entrance.

His last chance, this evening, was to join Rico and the oth-ers at Ménilmontant station. They must all be wondering where he'd been since the morning. They might have some-thing for him to eat. Or some wine to drink. Wine kept you warm the longest. Better than coffee, milk, chocolate, any of that crap.

A nice big glass of wine, a smoke, and then he'd figure out where to spend the night. He just had to get there before they broke up and went off to their shelters or their crash pads. In particular, he hoped Rico would still be there. After all, Rico had been his buddy for the last two years.

Titi took a first cautious step, then another one. He shuffled his feet over the icy asphalt. The driver of the car waiting at the lights, probably amused at the awkward way Titi was walking, flashed his headlights and revved up his engine.

"Asshole!" Titi stammered, but without turning to look at the car for fear of slipping, falling and breaking his bones.

Pleased to have gotten across, he dove into the metro, only to be surprised that the warmth of it didn't hit him in the face the way it usually did. The corridors seemed as cold as every-where else. He started shivering again. He pulled his coat tight over his chest and sat down.

"Got a smoke?" he asked a young couple.

But he must have spoken too softly. Or maybe he hadn't spoken at all, only in his head. The couple kept on walking along the platform without even looking at him. He watched them kissing and laughing.

A train finally arrived.

"Where the fuck were you?" Dédé asked.

Of the five Ménilmontant regulars, he was the only one still there.

"Rico waited for you all this time. He's gone to look for you at the shelter. I was just leaving."

Titi nodded. No sound came from his lips.

"Titi, you O.K.?"

With his fingers, Titi mimed the action of eating. "Hungry," he said. At least, he thought the word came out.

"Shit, Titi, I don't have anything. Anything at all! Not even a drink."

The light went out in Titi's eyes. His eyelids closed, and he dozed off. Changing trains at Belleville had exhausted him. He'd almost fallen on the stairs a few times.

"Fuck, Titi, you sure you're O.K.?"

Titi nodded.

"I have to go, Titi. Here . . ."

Dédé took a crumpled cigarette from his pocket, smoothed it between his fingers, then lit it and put it between Titi's lips. His eyes half closed, Titi slowly breathed in the smoke, and moved his head up and down. His way of saying thank you.

"I'll tell him you're still here, O.K., Titi? Do you hear me? Don't worry, they'll come for you."

Dédé gave Titi a friendly pat on the shoulder, then disappeared under the sign saying *Change for Nation-Porte Dauphine line*. The platform was deserted. Titi continued smoking, the cigarette between his lips, his eyes closed. He dozed off again.

The arrival of a train made him jump. Several people got off, mostly from the middle of the train, but no one noticed him. Titi took a last drag on what was left of his cigarette, then threw it away. He was shaking more and more.

He got heavily to his feet and dragged himself to the end of the platform. There, he slid behind the row of plastic seats, lay down on his side, facing the wall, pulled his coat collar over his head, and closed his eyes.

The winter inside him had won.

PART ONE

1.

"ON THE ROAD AGAIN, FOREVER"
TITI USED TO SAY

Rico refused to answer any questions from the journalists. He had been the first of their little group of down-and-outs to come back to Ménilmontant station, early in the afternoon. The southbound platform, where they usually met, was sealed off. So he went and sat down on the opposite platform.

There were no trains running. The place was swarming with people. Firefighters with their resuscitation equipment, police, officials from the transit authority. When Rico saw them taking Titi away, he knew he was dead.

A TV crew arrived. Local news. The reporter, a young woman with an austere face and short, almost crew-cut hair, spotted him, and in a few minutes the crew was all over him. He hadn't had the strength to move. He was too sad.

Titi was dead.

"About Titi," the reporter said. "That's what they called him, isn't it?"

He continued smoking, eyes downcast, and didn't reply. He had nothing to say. What was there to say? Nothing. After all, as the head of security for the transit authority was to tell the same reporter, "At this time of year, homeless people die in the metro almost every day, several a week anyway, especially of heart attacks . . ."

That evening, Rico watched the TV news at an Arab café on Rue de Charonne called Abdel's. He was a regular there. He would have a beer and a smoke and watch TV, and no one ever came over and told him he was upsetting the customers. Abdel sometimes gave him a plate of couscous.

"Did you know the guy they're talking about?" Abdel asked.

"He was a friend of mine."

"Damn! God rest his soul."

What had surprised Rico was how precise the reporter had been in her opening remarks. "Jean-Louis Lebrun died at the age of 45 on the platform at Ménilmontant metro station on Friday January 17 at about ten or eleven in the evening. His body was not removed until the following day, Saturday January 18, at two-thirty in the afternoon. Hundreds of Parisians passed by without seeing a thing. So did transit authority staff."

"That's disgusting," Abdel commented.

"When you consider the millions of people using the metro, it's not so surprising . . ." the transit authority spokesman had said.

"Another beer?"

"Sure."

Then Dédé appeared on the screen.

Dédé had come onto the platform, yelling about how the transit authority had let Titi die. "It's true, before I left I told the guy at the ticket office. I told him Titi wasn't looking well. I mean, he was sick, right? I thought they were going to call the fire department, and . . ."

The journalist had made him repeat it all, more calmly, for the cameras. Naturally, the station supervisor stated that the man doing the night shift hadn't been told.

"Of course," the spokesman concluded, all smiles, "we usually make sure that no one is left inside the stations during the night. But out of the goodness of their hearts, our supervisors sometimes turn a blind eye. That must have been what happened last night."

Rico had stopped listening. He was sipping his beer and thinking about Titi. Titi who'd been his friend for the past two years. His only friend. The last one.

They had met outside the hall belonging to the church of Saint-Charles de Monceau, standing in line on the sidewalk with about twenty others. As far as food was concerned, they said it was the best you could find in Paris. In addition, the cook, Madame Mercier, liked to dress up her dishes with fancy names. A pile of noodles sprinkled with sausage meat, served in a plastic bowl, for example, would be down on the menu as *timbale of pasta in meat sauce*!

Since he'd discovered the place, Rico had gone there often, the way normal people go to a restaurant. Not too often, though, because before eating, you were expected to meditate for two minutes, then pray. Always an Our Father, followed by stupid prayers to Saint Vincent de Paul, "the friend of the poor," Our Lady of Good Counsel, and a whole series of saints that Rico didn't give a damn about.

But having to listen to all that crap wasn't the worst of it. The really stupid thing was that you had to pick up a ticket an hour and a half before they served the meal. Then the parish priest, Father Xavier, would offer catechism lessons—"only to those who want it, of course." Obviously, if you took up the offer, you were one of the first to sit down at the table and discover Madame Mercier's dish of the day.

One evening, Rico had resigned himself to following the priest. A sermon, a hymn, was better than being left out. Cod *à la provençale* was on the menu, and Rico couldn't remember the last time he'd eaten cod. It was a hellish hour, a grim reminder of his childhood and compulsory religious lessons. Father Xavier had finished his lesson with the words, "Yes, my brothers, Christ would happily have eaten pig swill, but no one gave him any." By this point, Rico had felt as if he was about to scream. Since then, even though he'd enjoyed Madame Mercier's cod, he'd avoided the catechism lessons.

The day Rico and Titi met was the day before Easter.

Behind them, about thirty men and women had joined the line. The door of the church hall was still closed, so they couldn't even get their meal tickets.

After they'd waited at least an hour, Father Xavier had finally come out and explained what was happening. The hall would be closed that Thursday and on Good Friday too.

"Those of us who believe in Jesus Christ," he had begun, "—and I know not everyone does, but never mind—must remember that Our Lord died for us this Easter weekend."

They had all bowed their heads, thinking, O.K., let's get the Easter sermon over with.

The priest had cleared his throat. "We won't be serving any meals today or tomorrow. We Christians are celebrating the last meal Jesus shared with his disciples . . ."

"Come on!" Titi had muttered. "He gets a last meal, and we go without."

"Amen, brother, and tighten your belt," Rico had replied, laughing.

They had looked at each other and, without waiting for the end of the priest's oration, had left. In search of another place to find food.

"Rue Serrurier," Rico had suggested.

"Too many people. And it's too far to go this time of night."

"Rue de l'Orillon, then . . ."

"Are you kidding? That place gives you diarrhea. I've been on the street for six years, and I've made a note of all the places where I caught something. I avoid them if I can. No, we'll try the Trinité. Not exactly three stars, but decent-sized portions . . . And full of really cute girl students with skirts up above their knees. That certainly helps the congealed rice go down!"

They had both laughed, and since then they had been inseparable.

Titi and Rico never told each other how they'd ended up on

the street. They both sensed that, even though there might be a few differences, their stories were similar. So, whenever they sat down to have a smoke, they preferred to talk about all kinds of other things. Especially Titi.

Rico reckoned Titi must have been a teacher, a professor, something like that. He'd read lots of books and was always referring to them in their conversations. One afternoon, they were sitting on a bench in the sun, on Square des Batignolles—one of their favorite meeting places—and Titi had said, "You know, when I was a teenager, I read a lot of Burroughs, Ferlinghetti, Kerouac . . ."

Rico responded with a blank expression.

"Haven't you ever read *On the Road*?"

Rico had not read anything since his school days. Well, maybe a few pulp thrillers sometimes. Not that there'd been any shortage of books in his house. A whole bookcase full of them. Bound volumes with illustrated covers, which arrived every month in the mail. Sophie had taken out a subscription. She thought it was good to have books in the house. Stylish, she said. But she didn't read either. She preferred women's magazines.

"No. I don't really know much about books . . ."

"These guys were beatniks. You must have heard of beatniks?"

"Yes . . ."

As far as Rico was concerned, beatniks were just guys with long hair, flowery shirts and guitars slung over their shoulders. He remembered the singer Antoine. And Joan Baez. Peace and love, that kind of thing. Not really his style. At the age of sixteen, he was more the clean-cut type, always dressed to the nines. He'd have liked to spend his life zooming around in a red Ferrari.

"Those guys, the American beatniks, the real ones I mean, used to hitchhike all over the States. Living like bums, living wild . . . This bozo Kerouac wrote a book about their adventures called *The Dharma Bums*. He thought they were on a spiritual quest."

Rico had smiled. "Well, I don't see anything spiritual on our road."

Titi had been silent for a moment. Then he'd said, "On the road again. That was their motto." He was staring into the distance. "On the road again," he had repeated, pensively. "What bullshit!"

Both of them knew their road wasn't a road anymore. More like a swamp, and they were sinking into it, a little more every day. There was nothing they could do about it. Even if someone managed to grab hold of their hands, it was too late. The hands reaching out to them weren't reaching out in friendship. Not anymore. They were just handing out charity. A cup of hot coffee. A can of corned beef. A portion of processed cheese.

"On the road again, forever, that's us, Rico."

"Yeah."

"Fucking jerks!"

"Fucking jerks," Rico muttered, finishing his beer.

On the screen, the presenter had moved on to the dramatic story of hundreds of motorists on their way back from ski resorts, who had been trapped on the roads by heavy snow. All the emergency services were out in force in the Alps to help these unfortunate families in distress.

Rico smiled. Maybe Sophie was stuck in the snow. Sophie and Alain, Éric and Annie . . .

"Fucking jerks," he muttered again, standing up.

Abdel wouldn't take any money for the beers. "Come back whenever you like. It's warm in here."

Rico pulled the zip of his sweater right up to his mouth, buttoned up his military greatcoat, pulled his hat down over his ears, thrust his hands deep in his pockets, and went out into the cold. According to the weather reports, the temperature was expected to go down to below 14° Fahrenheit.

The icy air hit him, as pale as the light from the street lamps. This evening, he told himself, he'd eat at the Salvation Army on the corner of Rue Faidherbe. For ten francs, he knew he'd get his fourteen hundred calories.

He felt a sudden lump in his throat. He wanted to cry. Titi! he screamed inside his head. Titi. He remembered the corpse being carried away. Titi, him, the others, they were nothing. Nothing. That was the only fucking truth in this life. He started walking faster.

2.

MEMORIES JUST MAKE YOU CRY

T hat night, Rico decided to leave Paris. If he was going
to die, he might as well die in the sun. That's what
he'd told himself.

All these things that had been going around and around in
his head ever since he had seen the firefighters taking Titi's
body away boiled down to one inescapable fact: he'd end up
like Titi. It was an illusion to think he could still pull through,
could still lead some kind of life on the street.

Compared with some, of course, he wasn't too bad off. He
had a good crash pad. A few bar owners treated him well, a few
street traders at the Aligre market. And when he opened the
door to customers at the post office on Rue des Boulets, people took pity on him and gave him money. But it wouldn't last
forever. One of these days, he'd go under. Because one of these
days, he wouldn't have any strength left to do anything. In fact,
he hadn't had much strength left since this afternoon. It was
force of habit that had kept him going, not will power.

He lay on his back and lit a cigarette. He felt a gnawing in
his stomach. It must be five o'clock. Hunger was the most
accurate alarm clock there was. He remembered something
Titi had told him. "You know, Rico, when I was a kid, I
thought hunger was like a toothache, only worse. After a while,
I mean. Since being on the street, I've come to realize that
hunger's no big deal. It's easier to handle than a toothache!"
Rico smiled. Titi had long since lost his teeth, one after the
other!

He grabbed the bottle of vodka from behind him and took
a long swig. He'd haggled over that bottle at an all-night Arab

grocery on Faubourg Saint-Antoine, and had finally gotten it for seventy-five francs. It was Smirnoff. He'd had this craving for spirits when he left the Salvation Army. The dish of salt pork and lentils he'd eaten had assuaged his hunger, but not his grief. Nor his sense of dread. Titi's death had broken down all the barriers he'd patiently put up between his present life and his past life.

Rico grimaced. As always happened when he drank on an empty stomach, the liquid felt sticky in his throat. He coughed, got his breath back, and took another gulp. He closed his eyes and waited to feel the warmth of the vodka in his body, then took a drag on his cigarette, and tried again to think things through. Turning things over and over in his head was all he'd done all night.

Rico's crash pad was on the corner of Rue de la Roquette and Rue Keller. In a building under construction. Like so many working-class areas, the neighborhood was being gentrified, and they were tearing down old buildings left, right and center, to build luxury apartment blocks. Renovation, they called it in city hall.

Always on the lookout, Rico had ventured onto the construction site late one afternoon six months before. Six stories were already finished, but work seemed to have stopped. In the basement, he discovered the parking garage. Partitioned into individual spaces. He settled down in one of them for the night, on a tarp—if you folded it properly, it made for an excellent mattress. For the first time in ages, he slept the sleep of the blessed.

At six o'clock, a security guard found him. A tall black guy, all muscle under an impeccable blue uniform. There was a badge sewed on the left pocket, with the words *Paris Security*.

"What are you doing here?"

"Sleeping."

"No trespassing, man. Can't you read?"

"No trespassing, but it doesn't say anything about no sleeping," Rico joked, collecting his few things together.

"Where are you going?"

"Getting out of here, right?"

The security guard offered him a cigarette and lit it for him.

"Dunhill! Shit, it's been a long time."

"There's no rush, man. You can stay."

They stared at each other as they puffed happily at their cigarettes.

"It won't bother me, O.K.?"

The security guard, a Madagascan named Hyacinthe, told him that the construction company had gone bankrupt. A buyer had been found for the company, but it would be a while before the work started again.

Rico settled in. He went to the Gare de Lyon and fetched all his things from the two lockers where he'd left them: his backpack, a sleeping bag, some clothes, a small camp stove, a few candles, a china cup and a few other knick-knacks he'd picked up over the years. When he woke up, he would put everything away under the tarp he used at night for a mattress.

Every morning, Hyacinthe bought Rico a coffee and a croissant at Bébert's, a bistro a bit farther along the street that remained resolutely unfashionable in this hot new Parisian neighborhood.

"I was a security guard at this superstore out in the suburbs," Hyacinthe said. "One afternoon, I spot a guy like you . . ." He sipped at his coffee. "Don't get upset, O.K., Rico? I'm just saying, it was my job to keep my eyes open."

"I know."

"The guy was pushing a trolley with a six-pack of beers and a loaf of bread in it. I see him stop at the delicatessen counter. He asks for a slice of ham and a little pâté, then carries on along the aisles . . ."

"And starts eating!"

"You said it, man!"

"I've done that sometimes."

"When I saw him again, he was in the electrical section, glued to the TV sets. Bread and pâté, bread and ham . . . I left him alone. Then, as cool as a cucumber, he went to the checkout and paid for his six-pack and . . . that evening they fired me. The guy in charge of the delicatessen counter had informed on me."

"The jerk!"

"Places like that are full of jerks. The same guys who can't stand blacks and Arabs . . ."

"What are you doing as a security guard?"

"It's the only thing I know. I can hardly read or write, man. Hey, this is a more honest job than being one of those Rambo types who work for the transit authority!"

When construction work started again in the fall, Hyacinthe reassured Rico. There was no need to worry. The parking garage would be the last thing they touched. Rico just had to get his things out of the way before the workers arrived, so as not to get Hyacinthe into trouble. And as they didn't arrive too early, Rico could still have a lie-in.

For some time now, his thoughts had been out of control. They came in waves, in no particular order, and he found it hard to focus on a single one.

The cigarette had started to burn his fingers, and he clung to the memory of his last fixed abode. Three years ago, when he was living with Malika. Not that he was eaten up with desire for Malika right now. He didn't feel anything physical for her anymore. Or for Julie. Or even for Sophie, even though he'd been madly in love with her. Women belonged to another world now. As inaccessible as a major blow-out in an expensive restaurant.

"How do they do it?" Titi had asked, eyeing up a pretty

brunette pacing up and down the platform, waiting for the metro.

She was wearing a miniskirt under her open coat.

"Do what?"

"Wear skirts up to here without freezing."

"I guess it warms up their pussies to know they're getting us all excited," Rico had joked.

"I guess so . . ."

Not that Rico was excited. Even imagining himself slipping his hands between the girl's thighs didn't give him a hard-on. He hadn't jerked off for ages. His dick stayed limp, whatever images of women he conjured up. Even the image of Sophie offering him her ass so that he could take her doggie-fashion. After a while, the flaccid piece of flesh between his fingers sickened him. He disgusted himself.

"You know something?" Titi had resumed, without taking his eyes off the brunette. "We'd need to eat at least ten rare steaks to be able to fuck a girl like that."

She walked back past them, slowly.

"Any chance of a smoke for me and my buddy?" Titi had asked.

She had shrugged, indifferently.

"We're not her type, old pal."

This was what they'd come to. Impotent even for life.

Rico stubbed out his cigarette and took another long swig of vodka. He was starting to feel warm inside. There was nothing else like it to help you think.

He'd never felt any resentment against Malika. Everyone had his own life to live. And there always came a moment when you knew you had to save your own skin. That was what she had done. They'd been living together for two years. On Rue Lepic. In a little two-room seventh-floor apartment overlooking a courtyard. Malika worked as a switchboard operator for some company out in Issy-les-Moulineaux. He'd never discovered what its name was. He'd found a job working for a porn dealer, delivering what he assumed were hard-core videos to ritzy neighborhoods in Paris.

Things were fine between him and Malika. It wasn't happiness, but it was O.K. He was living a normal life, like the people he passed on the street. Not like before, when he'd lived with Sophie, but normal enough to make you believe that it was possible to start all over again and rebuild your life.

One day, someone stole his moped. His boss refused to provide him with a new one. "You deal with it. No moped, no work. I can't afford a moped for every idiot that comes along. The next person I hire has to have his own transportation. I'll make it a condition. Either you find a moped by this time tomorrow, or you're out . . ."

"Go fuck yourself!"

He dug his heels in. After that, he couldn't find another job. His relationship with Malika became strained. It was harder and harder for the two of them to live on his welfare payments.

Time passed. A year. The welfare payments ran out, and he spent his time hanging out in bars. One evening, he came home, fairly drunk as usual, to find the apartment empty. Malika had left, taking almost all their things with her. She hadn't even left him a note. "O.K.," he'd thought. "It's not the end of the world." And he'd gone out again and had a few more drinks, on Place Blanche.

Rico kept the apartment. The rent arrears accumulated. The registered letters. The notifications of eviction. The day before he was due to be thrown out, he left of his own accord, taking only some clothes and a few odds and ends that soon turned out to be useless on the street. He'd long ago sold the few things Malika had left behind. Including what belonged to the landlord. The little fridge and the hotplate in the kitchenette.

It was the end of May. The air was fragrant with spring.

Rico slept that night in the open air, on Square Henri IV. The first morning was like a new dawn of happiness. Of freedom. He had turned a page. He was setting off into the unknown. After those wretched years with Malika, he felt liberated.

He was starting a new life, with his rucksack on his back. He felt like a tourist in Paris. He blew sixty francs on a nice big breakfast on Place du Châtelet: fruit juice, coffee, croissants, bread and butter. Leaving the bar, he told himself that life on the street wasn't going to be as hard as all that. He was in top form, wasn't he? The city was his.

When Titi had told him about the beatniks, Rico hadn't said anything, but he'd remembered that first morning. On the road again, you said it, what bullshit! And forever, dammit! Because six months later, it was obvious to Rico that it really was forever. He realized that the things he'd taken with him were of absolutely no use. He'd been so convinced that the situation wouldn't last, he'd neglected the really important things—good shoes, a penknife, a nail file, a sleeping bag.

And then there were the souvenirs.

"Crap," Titi had said. "You carry all these letters and photos around with you. All they do is make you cry. It's bad for morale. If you're going to burn your bridges, then burn them. You have to choose."

He'd thrown everything away. Sophie's letters, their photos. The only thing he'd kept was a photo of Julien. An ID photo. He could forget everything, but not his son.

Hyacinthe woke him.

"Shit, Rico, what are you doing here, man? Have you seen what time it is? They're coming in."

Rico was in a daze.

"Get all that stuff out of the way right now."

Hyacinthe was angry. For the first time, Rico had broken their agreement.

"Sorry," he said, getting to his feet.

"Hurry up!"

Rico didn't put anything away. He just shoved it all under the tarp. Right now, he didn't give a fuck about anything, even Hyacinthe. At last he knew where to go. A place to die.

"I'm leaving, Hyacinthe. I'm getting out of here."

"Don't talk bullshit. I didn't say anything."

"It's not that. In two days at the latest, I'm going, and that's it. You won't see me anymore. I'm going south. To Marseilles. Marseilles," he repeated, with delight.

That's where I met Rico. In Marseilles. And that's where I learned everything I know about him and about that shitty life, where everyone is alone and defeated from the start.

3.

IN WHICH WE GLIMPSE THE BITTERNESS
AND GREATNESS OF DREAMS

Marseilles. In Rico's restless, painful sleep, images of Marseilles had resurfaced. Slowly at first. Then in waves. Streets, squares, bars. The sea, the beaches, the white rock . . .

These memories were like picture postcards sent him by the past. As if the past had finally found his address, and was forwarding mail that hadn't been distributed for fifteen years. Greetings from Marseilles. Best wishes from Marseilles.

"I love you, Léa."

"I love you too."

Léa.

Her image came to the fore early in the morning, when Rico fell asleep again after finishing the bottle of vodka. Nostalgia for a lost happiness. A feeling that, perhaps, his life had taken the wrong turn the day he'd decided to marry Sophie instead of Léa.

When he met her, Léa was just starting an architecture course. He'd not long arrived in Marseilles, after finishing his military service in Djibouti, in the marines. He and his friends in the regiment were waiting in the camp at Sainte-Marthe, north of the city, to be demobilized.

Late one afternoon, strolling aimlessly before meeting up with his buddies for another night on the town, he got lost in a maze of alleys.

Léa was taking a photograph of the front of an old building. She had her back to him. Loose-fitting beige linen pants, a roomy light gray sweater that covered her buttocks, her head a mass of curly black hair.

He went up to her. "Excuse me."

She turned, and the beauty of her face took his breath away. Deep-set dark eyes. A thin nose. High cheekbones. Well-defined crimson lips.

"Yes?"

"Er . . . I'm sorry," he said, unsettled. "Could you tell me how to get to the Vieux-Port?"

She looked at him in surprise, a slight smile on her lips. "You're lost, is that it?"

There was irony in the question. Cheekiness too.

"Yes . . . I'm not from around here."

She burst out laughing at his honesty. "But it's impossible to get lost in this city! All the streets lead down to the sea."

"Well, that may be . . . But . . . well, I just couldn't find the right one!"

She laughed again, and Rico fell in love with her laugh. "I'm going down there myself. It's not very far."

It was an invitation.

He followed her without a word. They walked side by side in silence. She moved quite fast, her head held high, her eyes alert. Léa barely came up to his shoulder and several times he felt like putting his arm around her. But he didn't. Hitting on women wasn't his style.

"Are you a photographer?" he asked, daring to break the silence.

"No, but I like it. How about you?"

"Like everyone else. Click, click."

There was a slight smile on Léa's lips, and Rico sensed her looking at him out of the corner of her eye.

"There you are!" she said, at the bottom of Rue Fort-Notre-Dame.

The Vieux-Port was there in front of them, bathed in the

light of the setting sun. A beautiful pale ocher light, typical of spring.

"I like this town."

"I love it!" Léa cried.

Rico asked if he could buy her an aperitif in the Bar de la Marine, and she said yes. They drank *pastis* and nibbled chick-peas and spicy black olives and talked a little about themselves. Rico told her proudly about the year he'd spent in Djibouti. The landscapes, the colors, the smells. The desert, Lake Assal, Lake Abbe. The caravans leaving for Ethiopia . . . He still hadn't gotten over it.

"I love those countries," Léa said.

I love. I hate. Léa wasn't one of those neutral people, always sitting on the fence, always taking other people's opinions into account in order to please them, to win them over. Rico was under her spell, ready to share all Léa's passions.

She'd already been to Egypt. She dreamed of traveling to Jordan and Yemen. Maybe even farther, to Asia Minor. And Armenia, "my family's poor country." She looked at him. "But not alone . . ."

Rico grabbed the opportunity. "Let's go tomorrow."

She burst out laughing, and, once again, Rico told himself he could spend the rest of his life listening to her laugh.

They met every evening for an aperitif, until he was finally demobilized. They exchanged addresses, promising to keep in touch. Rico wrote to her as soon as he got back to Rennes, and continued writing every day. Léa's letters soon started arriving just as regularly, and their correspondence changed. After a while, they stopped pretending to be just friends and started writing open love letters.

Come was the one-word message on the back of a postcard from her, a few months later.

It was the end of June. The only job Rico had been able to

find, as a traveling salesman for a German raincoat manufac-
turer, was not due to start until September.

He set off for Marseilles.

On the platform of Saint-Charles station, the two of them
were shy with each other at first. It's never an easy thing to put
words into actions. Léa's sparkling black eyes looked deep into
his. Rico finally took her in his arms, and their kiss was as passionate as their letters. "My Armenian doll," he whispered in
her ear: the words he used to start his letters.

They were both awkward that night. Rico's only sexual
experiences had been with prostitutes, in Rennes, then in the
army. And it was Léa's first time. It was over quickly, and probably neither of them enjoyed it very much. But then they lay in
each other's arms for a long time, without talking. There was
surprise and joy in Léa's eyes, Rico thought—incredulity too.
He was thrown. Love, he was starting to discover, was about a
whole a lot more than just sleeping with someone.

"It's nice here with you," Léa murmured.

She gently pulled the sheet over them, and fell asleep, or at
least pretended she had. He did the same, but in his case he
really did fall asleep.

"What would you like?" she asked him when he opened his
eyes the next morning.

"Whatever you're having."

"Black coffee, then. It's ready."

From the window of Léa's little two-room apartment on
Rue Neuve-Sainte-Catherine, right near the Abbaye Saint-
Victor, there was a view out over the Vieux-Port.

"Down there is the Canebière, can you see? And straight
ahead of you, the Fort Saint-Jean. I love it. It's so beautiful in
the sun. Behind it, you can see the bell tower of Les Accoules.
We can go there today, if you like."

Rico held her tight. So often, in her letters, she had described day breaking over the city. That moment when the air becomes transparent, when, like a miracle, the roofs turn blue and the sea pink. He recognized it all, as if he'd always lived here. *You'll see*, she had written to him. *In Marseilles, there are hours of the day when it's good to feel like this: standing here, halfway between the light and the sea. A way of knowing why we're from here and not from somewhere else, why we live here and nowhere else.*

That was now, Rico had thought.

The rest of his time there was a whirlwind. The exuberance of Marseilles seized him by the throat. More intensely, it seemed to him, than during his brief stay in the spring. People spoke loudly, they laughed and shouted all the time, they hooted their horns.

On Place des Moulins, in the Panier—the old quarter, near the harbor—Rico discovered that Marseilles was a city of hills. Léa and he had climbed the steps of Montée des Accoules.

"It's only when you walk, when you stroll around like this, that you realize quite how hilly this place is."

Until then, Rico had thought there was only one real hill, the one topped by the church of Notre Dame de la Garde—known as the Good Mother of the people of Marseilles—which was on all the picture postcards.

"That's how Marseilles deceives your sense of perspective," Léa remarked, showing off her architectural knowledge.

Rico felt the city taking possession of him. As gently as Léa's hands had taken possession of his body the previous night. He suddenly wanted to make love to her, right here, in one of these narrow alleys heavy with shadows, history, laughter and cries. These alleys that he loved, with their singsong names: Rue du Refuge, Rue de Lorette, Rue des Pistoles, Rue du Petit-Puis . . .

When they were on Place de Lenche, a violent storm suddenly broke, and they rushed back to Léa's apartment. Soaked to the skin and laughing like children. Their first siesta in Marseilles. Their bodies were in perfect harmony, and their pleasure was as sweet as it can be when you're first in love. It was as if Marseilles had carried them away, transported them.

Rico still had a vivid memory of the almost transparent blue light that came in through the window when the storm was over.

One day, they caught a bus. Léa wanted to show him the eastern outskirts of the city. The little ports of Les Goudes and Callelongue. The bus took the sea road. Once past the Catalan beach, Vallon des Auffes, Malmousque, the Fausse-Monnaie bridge, the whole harbor of Marseilles came into view. Vast and beautiful. Like a gift. Léa's gift to their love.

They changed buses twice. After Madrague de Montredon, the dry white rock made him wonder if he was still in the city. He couldn't get over it. It reminded him of the Aeolian islands where his parents had taken him when he was a child.

"The land of the Big Blue," Lea said proudly, pointing to the Riou archipelago.

The noise of the city, its exuberance, ended here. The silence that descended on them, disturbed only by the faint chug-chug of the fishing boats returning from the open sea, was so intense, you could touch it, smell it. It smelled of salt and iodine. Léa and Rico sat down behind an angler, and forgot all about time.

Léa had fallen silent. And now it was Rico who really wanted to say something. To tell her what he had loved about Marseilles. They gazed into each other's eyes, with a look of total love, *the kind of look in which we glimpse the bitterness and greatness of dreams*, as Léa was to write, recalling that moment, when Rico announced that it was all over, that he had met someone else. *Penelope and Odysseus must have looked at each other that way when they parted.*

But Rico only skimmed through that letter. His heart was in another place. With Sophie.

When Hyacinthe shook him to wake him up, Léa's voice was still in his head, asking, "What are you smiling about?"

"You. Marseille. Me. Us. Us being here."

They were on Rue Longue-des-Capucins. "Our own oriental market," she called it. A place where all the smells of the Maghreb, Africa, Asia merged into a single smell, as heady as happiness. The promise of happiness.

Rico hadn't dared to add, "Us always, maybe." He should have.

These unchanged memories, the only good memories he still had left, were well worth another journey to Marseilles. "If you're going to die," as Rico said to me, "you might as well die faithful to moments like that, don't you think?"

4.

WHAT'S INEXPLICABLE IS THAT YOU CAN HATE, AND STILL LOVE

Outside, it was snowing. A fine, cold snow that not even children wanted to play in. In the metro, people had even longer faces than usual. Rico got off at Ménilmontant to see his friends and tell them he was leaving.

"Where were you, for fuck's sake?" Dédé asked. "We haven't seen you for two days. We were worried, dammit!"

At the end of the platform, Jeannot, Fred and Lulu were having a picnic, huddled over two plastic boxes full of what looked like paella. Dédé was smoking, and watching them eat.

"Looks like a party," Rico joked.

"You know that food store?" Jeannot said. "The one on the boulevard, at the corner of Rue Oberkampf? The owner gave us this when Fred and I passed by at noon."

"Apparently, they talked about us on TV last night," Fred said. "They said there are hundreds of us dying of cold and hunger on the streets of Paris . . ."

"Seems it made the owner's wife cry when she saw it. So . . . Want some?" Lulu asked, holding out a plastic spoon.

Rico shook his head. "I'm not hungry."

He hadn't eaten anything since the previous evening. He'd tried, but nothing would go down. Not even a cookie. There was a knot of pain in his stomach. Too much grief. Too much sadness. He could only handle a liquid diet. Beer and cheap wine. A few cups of coffee.

Dédé laughed. "The thing is, if we all start dying this winter, there'll be a hell of a mess on the streets! Am I right, guys?"

The three others laughed too.

Dédé was always saying things like that. He was a bit of a

loudmouth, and his irony and cynicism sometimes irritated Rico. But he liked him all the same. Titi had liked him too.

The three of them had always gotten along. That must have been because, even if they didn't exist anymore in the eyes of society, they weren't resigned to accepting just anything that came along. Not like Jeannot, Fred and Lulu. You only had to see them wolfing down the food to realize that. That was why Titi had died. Because his dignity wouldn't let him fall any lower. He would never have touched that leftover paella.

Rico had often wished he'd met Titi earlier and had him as a friend for longer. He'd never have abandoned him. Not like the others, the people he'd believed in for years, who'd all made themselves scarce when things had started going wrong for him. Vincent, Philippe, Robert, and Éric.

Éric. His old school friend, his companion on so many wild nights. The best man at his wedding, who hadn't even called him when Sophie had left. Rico had wiped Vincent, Philippe and Robert from his memory. For good. But not Éric. There was no way he'd ever forgive him.

He should have known, though, that Éric would be that way. It had been on the cards for a long time. Éric believed in the good life. In a world where money goes hand in hand with family and happiness. The medical laboratory he had inherited from his father was doing well. He was surrounded by a good team. He did practically nothing and got well paid for it, invested his money wisely and got a good return.

Rico could still recall an argument they'd had one evening when they were eating out.

"I'm fed up to the teeth with all that humanitarian bullshit!" Éric had said, angrily. "You know as well as I do, these guys you see on the street are just assholes. Lazy assholes. If they wanted to work—"

"There's a recession, Éric. But you don't want to see that,

you don't want to know anything. Even in my profession, they're laying people off."

"Oh, no!" Éric's wife Annie had cried. "You're not going to start talking politics, are you? We get enough of that on TV . . ."

"You're right, darling. All the same, if they sent all the blacks and Arabs back home, there'd be room for all the French people who are having a hard time right now."

"Éric has a point," Sophie cut in. "But what I really want to know is, where are we going for the holidays? The West Indies, or to the mountains to ski?"

When they got back home, Rico quarreled with Sophie. Not because she'd supported Éric—he didn't give a damn what she thought—but because, as she must have known, their financial situation was far from being secure.

After Julien was born, Sophie had asked for time off from the bank where she worked. A woman's role, she had declared, was to take care of her child, to bring him up. She'd always been a bit of a conservative. But when Julien had started school, Sophie had decided not to go back to her job as a business consultant. She would be a housewife, like Annie.

Rico had started working even harder, making more and more trips out to the western end of his territory. A lot more money was coming in, of course. But even so, it wasn't easy to live in the same style as Éric and Annie. Especially as a large part of his income went into repaying the loan on the beautiful house they had bought at Rothéneuf, near Saint-Malo.

One afternoon, on their bench on Square des Batignolles, Rico had opened up to Titi about all these things. He was feeling down. It was the start of the school year, and he "wasn't there" for Julien. He always felt bad at this time of year. It was worse than Christmas. Not that he liked Christmas. Midnight mass, the family dinner, the tree, the presents, all that respectable hypocrisy.

"What'd be the point in your coming?" Sophie had replied when he had called. "We can live without you, fortunately."

In the divorce settlement—which came a whole year after Sophie left, because he had stubbornly refused to give her one—Rico had not even obtained visiting rights. He was a violent alcoholic. That was what Sophie's lawyer had managed to get the judge to swallow as the reason for his client having abandoned the marital home. All his friends' wives had agreed with that. Especially Annie. True, he had called Annie a hypocritical bitch. But he wasn't drunk that evening, just angry, and hurt.

Moved by Rico's story, Titi had also opened up a little, for the first time. Rico had understood what it was that united them. They had both believed in the same thing. They had both dreamed of love, a proper family, a good position in life. Security and stability too. And everything had collapsed, without their really knowing why.

"One day, I realized I didn't want to struggle anymore in order to succeed. Earn money, all that shit . . . You know, Rico, there are lots of good guys like us on the street. All I can say, after years of living this kind of life, is that when I look at the way society is, I don't have any particular desire to go back to it. Trust me, I'm never going back to their world."

Rico had often thought about what Titi had said. However hard he pondered Titi's words, he couldn't decide whether or not he wanted to go back to his former life. Until he had gone to Rennes, the previous day.

After leaving Hyacinthe, Rico had gone to the post office on Rue des Boulets to beg. His heart hadn't really been in it. But he had to make a little money. He couldn't get away from that.

And besides, begging had one advantage. It meant you didn't have to think. Rico had discovered that in order to open the door of the post office, hold out your hand, say hello, goodbye, thank you, thank you very much, goodbye, have a nice day, you needed to have a completely empty head.

"Once you start 'work,' you have to focus on an absolute minimum of words and gestures. To get the maximum number of coins dropping into your hand."

Titi had told him that, when Rico mentioned that he made barely sixty francs a day.

"Get this into your head, Rico. Once you hold out your hand to beg, you're admitting, once and for all, that you're out of the running, that you're in this life for good."

"I know."

Rico had put off that moment as long as he could. He had finally taken the plunge at six o'clock one morning, after spending twenty-four hours without a penny. That had made him realize that he'd hit rock bottom.

"I feel so ashamed."

"We've all felt ashamed. But if you don't get beyond that, you're dead, Rico."

The shame hadn't gone away. But he had found a way to drown his humiliation. Just to get himself started, he would drink at least a couple of pints of cheap wine, then a couple of cups of coffee to conceal the smell, and concentrate on each person who entered the post office. That way, he managed to make between a hundred and a hundred fifty francs for eight hours' "work." That day, he made a hundred fifty-eight francs. A good day to go see Julien, he had thought.

At the Gare Montparnasse, he had caught the next to last train for Rennes. In case a fucking ticket collector threw him off at Le Mans, he could still try his luck with the last train, which was an express from Le Mans to Rennes. But no ticket collector came by.

As he always did when he went to Rennes—about once a month—he had slept in the parking lot behind the haulage depot. No one had disturbed him, not the security guards, not the backpackers with their fucking dogs. In the morning, he had a coffee in the station canteen, then went to the restroom, where he washed his face and shaved.

At eight o'clock, he set off downtown, to Rue d'Antrain and the Collège de l'Adoration, the school where Sophie had enrolled Julien soon after they had separated and she had settled in Rennes. It was the school that Éric and Annie's children attended. And Armel, the daughter of Alain, the man Sophie was living with now.

He leaned against a wall opposite the entrance to the school and smoked two cigarettes. Sophie's car arrived. A white Golf GTI. He straightened up. Sophie double-parked—she always did that, whatever the traffic—not far from where he was standing.

Armel got out of the car, followed by Julien.

"Hello," Rico said.

Julien stared at him. Every time Rico turned up like this, Julien looked at him in the same way. It was a look he found impossible to interpret. There was no contempt in it, no tenderness, no joy, not even indifference. Nothing.

"Hurry up, Julien," Sophie cried.

She had got out of the car, ignoring Rico. She was holding Armel by the hand. Julien joined her. They crossed the street. Outside the school entrance, Julien and Armel kissed Sophie, then went inside. Julien did not turn around.

Rico walked up to Sophie. Her blue eyes looked daggers at him.

"I'm in a hurry."

Her blond hair cascaded over the collar of her beige cashmere coat, which was open in spite of the cold. She was wearing a white roll-neck sweater and a tight-fitting chestnut-colored skirt cut well above the knees, revealing her beautiful legs.

Rico couldn't help remembering Titi's question, the day he was eying up the girl in the miniskirt. "How do they do it?" Now Rico had the answer. They're happy, that's how. Happiness keeps you warm.

He was only a couple of feet from Sophie. She was as beautiful and desirable as ever. If she'd said "Come," he'd have followed her, forgetting all about how much she'd hurt him. Yes, he would have forgiven her. You could hate someone, and still love them. That was something he had never understood, and never would.

"I'm going away. You won't see me again."

"I think that's best for all of us."

She got back in her car and drove off.

Rico stood there in the middle of the road, feeling lost. A young woman came up to him.

"Here," she said, slipping a ten-franc coin into his hand, "get yourself something hot to drink."

And she ran to her car—a green Mitsubishi station wagon—also double-parked.

He was so stunned, he didn't move after the station wagon had gone. He squeezed the ten-franc coin in the palm of his hand. Harder and harder, until it hurt. Then he flung it down in the road.

"Bitch!" he cried at last.

The word was meant for Sophie. For all the Sophies in the world, who dressed in Chanel or Dior, and drove Rovers or Xsaras or station wagons, like that stupid cow with her ten francs!

How long was it since he'd last felt anger? Years. The years on the street. These three years of learning resignation. Indifference to other people. To the world.

Why be angry with the woman for her charity? Standing there, in the middle of the road, what he looked like was what he was. A homeless man. A bum. And it was all

Sophie's fault. Sophie was the one he was angry with. The only one.

"Bitch!"

Because of her coldness. Her contempt.

"Bitch!"

How could she forget how much they'd loved each other? How could she deny that he was the father of her child? How could she bring up Julien in total ignorance of him?

"Bitch," he said in a low voice, and started to cry.

It took Rico a long time to recover from that grim morning. He walked for hours around the center of town. He felt like a stranger, even though he had lived here for years. It was as if the town and its people were hostile to him.

At five-thirty, he was again outside the school. In the same place.

"I want to give him a hug," he said to Sophie, when she got out of the car.

She said nothing and crossed the street. When the children came out, she said something in Julien's ear and he saw her nodding in his direction. They started walking toward the car. Rico stepped forward.

"Do you want to give your father a hug?" she asked Julien.

He didn't reply. He didn't take his eyes off Rico. He had his mother's eyes. Blue eyes, which had once been so gentle.

Sophie opened the back door and Julien got in, followed by Armel, who had been standing motionless behind the two of them, staring at Rico as if he was a Martian.

"You see, he doesn't want to give you a hug."

Angrily, she drove off. Through the rear window, Rico thought he saw Julien turning to look at him. But he couldn't be sure.

5.

TOO MUCH NOISE FROM THE PAIN AND TEARS

Now Rico was freezing his balls off with Dédé in the entrance to an apartment building in Neuilly, and he hadn't the faintest idea how he'd gotten here. Everything he'd said and done in the last part of the day seemed to have vanished into a black hole.

He'd been looking at Jeannot, Fred and Lulu wolfing down the paella as if it was their last meal. That much he did remember. And he also remembered Dédé holding out the bottle of Valstar and asking him again, "Where were you, for fuck's sake?"

Rico had taken a long swig of beer, then lit a cigarette. He hadn't yet recovered from his day in Rennes. Julien's indifference. Sophie's contempt. It was as if his heart was in a vise. Remembering himself standing there in the middle of the road with that fucking ten-franc coin in the palm of his hand made his stomach heave as if he was about to vomit.

"I just bummed around, that's all . . . Titi's death," he had added, stupidly, as if that was an excuse.

"Fucking bastards! I told the TV people that transit authority guy left him to die."

"I know, I saw it on the news."

"And you know what? They replaced him."

"Who?"

"The bastard who was there the other night!"

Rico had regretted mentioning his friend's death. He hadn't come to talk about Titi. Just to announce that he was leaving. But the pain and tears were making too much noise in his head. He had grabbed the Valstar and taken another long swig.

Jeannot had been the first to belch. "*Insh'Allah!*"

Fred and Lulu had quickly done the same. It became a game. Like farting.

"Come on!" Dédé had said to Rico. "Let's have a coffee at Les Tonneliers. I'm paying."

"Where are you two going?" Fred asked.

"To get some air. We'll be back."

It was great at Les Tonneliers. A warm, smoky atmosphere, like a real neighborhood bistro, which seemed to belong to another era, another Paris.

"Poor Titi. To think he could still be here."

"I don't think so," Rico had murmured, more to himself than to Dédé.

"You don't think so? Is that what you said?"

"Yes . . . I'm sure Titi didn't want that. In his head. Don't you see? In his head, he'd decided it was over."

"Maybe so . . . But hell, he could have died in a hospital bed all the same. Somewhere clean . . . Instead of there, like a mangy dog . . ."

"Isn't that what we are? Mangy dogs?"

Dédé had shrugged.

"Titi went back to Ménilmontant to die," Rico had continued. "That station was his last home. The place where he met his friends . . . I'm getting out of Paris, Dédé."

"Hell, man, where are you going?"

"South. Marseilles."

Rico had seen the surprise in Dédé's eyes.

"You have something lined up down there?"

"No . . . Just a few good memories . . . But I can't stick around here anymore, it's too painful."

Dédé had nodded. "Want a smoke?"

He had Camels.

"Shit, good smokes."

"Hey, just because you have nothing doesn't mean you have to deprive yourself."

They had both laughed.

Rico didn't know how Dédé got by on the street. If he begged, or if he had a little job on the side. The one thing for sure was that, of the whole gang, he was the one who looked least like a bum. He wore what looked like an almost new black coat, over a black leather jacket and black corduroy pants. He was almost elegant.

The only thing he knew about Dédé was that he'd spent five years in the Foreign Legion, and then had worked as a sales manager for a printing works whose main customer was the Crédit Lyonnais bank. When the bank started having problems, the printing works downsized its workforce and he was one of the first to be fired. Dédé was the only member of staff not in a union.

"How are you getting down there?"

"By train. At night."

The high speed trains were too much hassle. They were O.K. for short distances like Paris-Rennes. But on long journeys, things often didn't work out so well. He'd talked about it with a few of the backpackers. As soon as the ticket collector spotted you, he made you get off at the first stop, where the cops were usually waiting for you. Often it was some of the passengers who told the ticket collector about you before he'd even come by to check the tickets.

"I'll come with you part of the way, if you like. An old friend of mine lives in Chalon. We can eat and sleep at his place. I also need a change of scenery."

Rico had liked the idea. It was always better not to travel alone.

"How about tonight? Is that O.K. with you? We'll meet at the Gare de Lyon. At the buffet, opposite the information desk. We'll find a train."

Rico's bag was ready. Under the tarp in his crash pad on Rue de la Roquette. That morning he'd said goodbye to

Hyacinthe and had insisted on paying for the coffee and croissants this time. To thank him. Bébert, who always heard what
they were saying, had offered them a calvados.

"Great!" Dédé replied. "How about a beer to celebrate?
Hey, it's like we were going on vacation, isn't it?"

They'd gone from coffee to beer, then from beer to spirits.
Dédé paid for every round. The warmth and the alcohol had
gradually gone to Rico's head. It assuaged his hunger, and
soothed his mind. The words had started to come more easily,
like when he used to talk to Titi. Rico had no idea what they
had talked about, especially not what he could have said to
Dédé. All he remembered was that after a while Dédé had said,
"Right, shall we go?"

"O.K.," Rico had replied. "I'll follow you."

Outside, it was already dark.

Now here they were in the entrance to this fucking building, on the corner of Rue Poincaré and a frontage road paral-
lel to Avenue de Neuilly, not far from Sablons metro station.
The snow had been falling more heavily, and was starting to
settle on the ground. Rico felt the cold go right through him
even though, apart from his eyes, none of his body was
exposed.

From his coat, Dédé took the half-bottle of rum he'd
bought as they left Les Tonneliers, and took a swig.

"What are we doing here, Dédé? Can you tell me that?"

"We're waiting, dammit! I already told you. Here!" He
held out the bottle.

Rico knocked back a mouthful, then two, then three. His
body temperature went up several degrees.

"But what are we waiting for, for fuck's sake?"

A red Clio drove slowly past them and parked a little way
up the street. A young man in a black parka got out and ran to
the ATM at the corner.

"That's what we've been waiting for. The fall guy! Come on!"

Quickly, they came up behind the young man. Rico heard the click of a pocket knife. Dédé placed the blade against the young man's neck.

"Watch the car and the street," he ordered Rico.

The young man hadn't moved a muscle.

"How much can you take out? Three thousand?"

He shook his head. "One thousand five hundred," he stammered.

"One thousand five hundred? That's pathetic!"

"It's all I have. I'm telling the truth. I'm a student and—"

"Go on, put the card in and ask for two thousand."

"It won't work." His voice was shaking.

"Do as I tell you, dammit!"

A message came up on the screen. "One thousand two hundred!" Dédé screamed. "Is that all you can take out?"

"I've already withdrawn two hundred and four hundred. I'm only allowed one thousand eight hundred a week."

Dédé sighed. "Shit, man! You hear that? He can only take out one thousand eight hundred a week! This is a guy who lives in Neuilly, dammit!"

The machine spat out the bills, which Dédé quickly pocketed.

"O.K., the woman who's with you, does she have a card as well?"

The young man summoned up enough courage to say, "Leave her alone."

"I don't think you understand. You see my friend here? He doesn't say much, but he has a bit of a temper. So now he's going to fetch your girlfriend, and as long as no one does anything stupid, everything's going to be all right." He turned to Rico. "O.K.! Go get her!"

Rico obeyed, mechanically. He was completely out of his depth. He'd have liked a swig of rum, but Dédé had taken the bottle back.

He opened the door of the car. Rock music hit him in the face. A guy was singing:

O.K., boys, let's go to hell
Just have to throw the dice in the air

"Follow me," Rico said to the girl.

His tone of voice was all wrong, more of an invitation than an order.

"What?"

Rico grabbed her wrist. It was warm and soft. So slender, his fingers encircled it. The touch of it gave him the shivers. A woman's skin. Images flooded into his mind. Sophie. The whiteness of her body. He increased the pressure slightly, just so that his fingers could be in more contact with her skin.

Every night I count the days
Every night I count the days

"What?" the girl repeated, panicking now.

"Come with me. And there's no point in screaming!" He had almost found the right tone now. "And bring your bag."

He pulled her over to the ATM.

"Jacques," she whined, when she saw Dédé's knife being held against her friend's neck.

"It's all right, Camille. Take out your credit card."

"Withdraw as much as you can," Dédé ordered.

"Nine hundred," Camille replied softly.

"Fuck, what is this place, skid row?"

The ATM wouldn't give out nine hundred francs. There were no hundred-franc bills left, and it would only dispense multiples of two hundred francs.

Dédé collected the four bills. "Take her back."

Rico walked Camille back to the car, but this time he didn't dare grab her wrist. He squeezed her arm instead. He opened the door for her.

"Have a nice evening," he said.

He meant it. He looked at her one last time, then slammed the door. When he straightened up again, he realized that he was gasping for breath.

Dédé appeared, pushing Jacques in front of him and carrying Jacques' black parka under his arm.

"Now get out of here, and don't try anything stupid, like calling the cops on your fucking cellphone. I have your name and address. I can find you again, trust me."

Jacques put the car into first gear, stalled, restarted the engine, and finally managed to drive away.

"Here, present for you," Dédé said, handing the parka to Rico. "I saw right away it was your size."

"You're crazy, you know. Completely crazy."

"Don't jerk me around, Rico. Let's go."

"I'll walk. I need to walk, Dédé."

His breath was coming in rapid, wheezing gulps, as if he had just climbed the Himalayas.

"Hey, you O.K.?"

"Don't worry. Ten o'clock, Gare de Lyon."

"I'll be there. We'll divide up the money then."

Dédé went down into the metro and was gone.

Rico started walking slowly down the street. He had an intense pain in the small of his back, on the right hand side. A month earlier, a doctor from Médecins du Monde had diagnosed pleurisy. But Rico hadn't gone back to have it treated.

He felt as if he was suffocating. He stopped in a doorway, and waited for it to pass. He'd never done anything like that in his life. Even when things had been really hard on the street, it had never occurred to him to mug anyone. What surprised him was that he felt no remorse, no shame for having robbed those two young people. Nothing seemed to matter anymore.

He wondered what Titi would have thought. If Titi were still alive, would he even have followed Dédé? No, of course not. No . . . Although maybe . . . Everything was getting mixed up in his head, as usual.

He thought again about the girl, Camille. The touch of her skin. That was what had really shaken him. The last woman he had touched was Malika. That was three years ago. Since then . . . Since then, women had kept coming back to the surface of his mind. The vivid memory of Léa. The desire he still felt for Sophie . . . The ghosts of his loves.

His breathing gradually returned to normal. The pain in his back was wearing off. He remembered what Dédé had said. "If you're going to travel, it's best to have a little money, don't you think?"

Of course, Rico had thought. Especially as he had barely fifty francs in his pocket.

"I don't like the idea."

"Shit, Rico, just come with me, and wait there nice and quiet. That's all you have to do, O.K.? We do it and then we go."

"O.K.," he'd said at last. "O.K. I'll go with you."

The softness of Camille's skin. If only for that, he'd been right to follow Dédé.

He suddenly realized how warm the parka, which he was holding against his stomach, really was. It was new, or almost new, with a hood folded into the collar. He took off his military greatcoat and put on the parka. He zipped it right up and pulled the hood over his head, without taking off his hat. Within a few seconds, he felt his whole body warm up. "Fantastic!" If Dédé gave him half the money, as he'd suggested, this would turn out to be his best day since that first night on the street.

6.

A NIGHT IN WHICH NO ONE GIVES A DAMN
ABOUT ANYONE ELSE

During the journey, Rico had a nightmare. He was strangling Sophie. It was the day after she'd announced her decision to leave him. "I've really thought long and hard about it."

Rico's nightmare began in the morning, very early. He was standing in the doorway. He couldn't bring himself to leave, just like that, without a word. As if they'd said everything that had to be said. After a slight hesitation, he walked back into the bedroom. He wanted to talk to Sophie again, tell her how much he loved her. But also to ask her to spend the week giving it some more thought. Not to rush into things. To take her time. What had happened between Alain and her didn't matter. All that mattered was them. Her, Julien and him. Their little family. Such a nice family. All these words were in Rico's mouth as he opened the bedroom door.

Sophie was sleeping peacefully, with a smile on her lips. She seemed so calm, so remote from all the drama. The proposed separation. The end of their marriage. The end of that life he had wanted, that life he had sacrificed everything for.

Then he was sitting on the edge of the bed, smoking a cigarette and watching her sleep. He liked watching her sleep. He often did that, especially when he woke in the middle of the night, anxious about something. He always felt the same emotion as he had when they were first together. The same love. The years of marriage hadn't changed anything. But this morning, seeing her sleeping like that, peaceful and smiling, blew a hole in all his certainties. Why was she smiling like that? What was she dreaming?

So he stubbed out his cigarette, and started shaking Sophie angrily. The humiliation of knowing he'd been deceived, knowing she'd cheated on him, had turned to rage.

"You were dreaming about him, weren't you, you bitch?" he screamed, spitting out the words

The first thing he saw in her eyes was fear. She wanted to scream. But she couldn't, because Rico's fingers were around her throat.

"Let go of me," she breathed.

He was sitting astride her now, pressing down with all his weight on her hips. She was struggling, throwing back the sheet and trying to push him off. He was strangling her, filled with hate but also enjoying it. There was terror now in Sophie's eyes. Her heavy, wonderfully white breasts jiggled from side to side under her pajama top. He wanted to rip it off her. To rip the sheet too. And to make violent love to her naked body. To fuck her to death.

Rico was still squeezing. He was becoming breathless. It was himself he was strangling. The more he squeezed Sophie's neck, the more he choked. Then it was as if he could see himself in a mirror. His eyes rolled upwards, his tongue hanging out. Dead, or almost dead. And in a corner of the mirror he could see Julien, crying and demanding his breakfast. But still he squeezed. With all his strength. Until he choked to death.

His mouth opened wide. Desperate for oxygen.

"Hey, Rico! That's enough!"

Dédé was shaking him.

"Fuck it, Rico!"

Gasping, he extricated himself from his nightmare. For some reason he didn't understand at that point, he didn't like the way Dédé was looking at him. Didn't like what he saw in his eyes. Like a nightmare version of himself.

"Here, have a drink," Dédé said, opening a can of beer.

They'd bought a twelve-pack at the station before getting on the train.

"Where are we?" Rico asked, taking a swig of the beer.

"How the fuck do I know? Fucking train's hardly moving." Rico lit a cigarette.

"Bad dream, huh?" Dédé said.

Rico nodded. He didn't want to talk. He wanted to dismiss those terrible images from his mind.

"We all have bad dreams," Dédé went on. "It's because of the way we live."

"Yeah."

Did our bad dreams, lodged deep inside our heads, or our hearts, catch up with us eventually? Rico wondered, without being able to answer, every time he had this nightmare. He didn't have it often—fortunately, because each time he choked himself more, and there wasn't always someone around to wake him, like Dédé on the train, or me, later, in Marseilles. All the same—and Rico was categorical about this—however much Sophie had hurt him, he'd never wanted to kill her. Not that evening, not later. Besides, things hadn't exactly happened the way they did in his nightmare.

Sophie had been distant toward him for months. Their marriage, Rico realized, was in a bad way. They never talked, except when everyday problems, often quite trivial, led to arguments. Most of the time, Rico would end up falling in with Sophie's point of view, and they would make up as best they could. Usually in bed. In spite of all the years that had passed, Rico desired her as much as ever. He loved her body. A luscious body, which had ripened with time, and which she kept in shape by going for long runs on the beach. When she made love, Sophie was not at all the well-behaved, slightly strait-laced middle-class woman she liked to appear in company. She was a wonderful lover, so greedy for pleasure that Rico was always surprised.

"Ah, those convent girls!" Titi had said once. "Trust me, they're incredibly hot!"

They were on their bench on Square des Batignolles, both very drunk.

"The more they go to church, the more they love fucking. Teresa's syndrome, I call it. Ever hear of Teresa of Avila and her ecstasies? A saint and a fucking sex maniac!"

Rico had started to giggle.

"You may well laugh . . . Ever since then, they've preferred their little Jesus in the nude! . . . It's like American women, you know, they're supposed to be such Puritans . . . Take their panties down, you'll soon see the other America. Two, three times a night, they want it . . . And the things they do . . .!"

"Stop!"

"Stop!" he'd yelled at Sophie.

They were arguing again. This time because he was adamant about not getting a housekeeper.

"You don't do anything all day."

She'd looked at him with contempt. "That's just like you."

"What do you mean by that?"

"I mean, I've always known it. That's all women are for you, cooking, housework . . . and sex."

It was obvious Sophie was being disingenuous. This quarrel, like all the others, was just a pretext to distance herself from him. To get used to the idea that everything was over. Maybe—although Rico always refused to believe it—Sophie even enjoyed being cruel to him at this time. At least until her affair with Alain. *That other love,* she wrote to him one day, *which has calmed me down.*

"Bullshit!" he had replied, raising his voice. "You want everything, Sophie, everything. But I can't afford everything. Not now. For fuck's sake, do you know how much in debt we are?"

She had smiled. With that surprising smile of hers, her lips curled, which she sometimes had when she was reaching an orgasm. A carnivorous smile. "I thought you'd landed a new contract."

Rico had become a sales representative for a number of ready-to-wear manufacturers. It was a job he hadn't really chosen and didn't like much, but doggedly continued with.

"It's not settled yet. And even if I do . . . I don't know how I'm going to manage with all that work . . ."

"Well, don't think I'm going to iron your shirts for you. I've had enough of all that!"

And Sophie had walked out of the living room, slamming the door. When Rico had gone to bed, calmer now, he hadn't made any move toward her. He'd had enough of always giving in to her.

"Sophie," he had murmured.

It was nearly a month since they'd last made love. Nearly a month since that quarrel. He had won the new contract, but it had meant going on the road every week. Nantes, Brest, Caen. The route never changed. His Bermuda triangle.

Sophie's body had stiffened when he touched her.

"Leave me alone."

"What's going on?"

She had lit the bedside lamp and sat up in bed.

"I'm in love with someone else."

She had drawn up her knees under her chin, then had turned her face to him. Her angelic face, gentle and luminous. Rico couldn't have said if what he saw in her eyes was sadness or pity.

"I'm in love with someone else," she had repeated gently. "I didn't know how to tell you. I didn't know how to tell myself. It's all happened so quickly . . . But we . . . we're finished, you understand? I'm in love with someone else."

"You don't love me anymore."

It wasn't a question. Just a desperate statement of fact.

Rico had gotten to his feet and without another word, without even looking at her, had walked out of the bedroom. In the living room, he had poured himself a whiskey. To help him think. Images and words had passed through his mind. In slow motion. The gestures she had made. The words she had said. Her hesitations too. Their silences. And sometimes, their tear-filled eyes.

Drinking one whisky after another, he had tried to convince himself that all was not lost, that everything was still possible. Sophie, *his* Sophie, loved him too, whatever she said. He had sensed it in the way she'd told him things, the way she'd put her hand on his. "You're such a good man, I know . . ."

He had fallen asleep on the couch, the bottle of whisky empty at his feet, and had woken with a start at about four in the morning. His mind was still turning over, like a machine. "I'm in love with someone else." Alain. She hadn't said his name, but he *knew* it was him. The only bachelor in their group. "You don't love me anymore." Her only response had been silence. Her face hidden by her mass of blond hair. Tired, his tongue coated, he'd had to face the truth. He had lost Sophie forever. He had dressed and left the house. He had driven like a madman. All the way to Nantes.

That was what had really happened that night. In the first bar he found open, Rico began his day with a cognac. By the third one, he knew his life had been turned upside down.

Rico was still silent, drinking his beer in small sips. Dédé was sitting opposite him. He wasn't saying anything either. Occasionally, they'd look at each other, then look away and stare out the window of the compartment, into the blackness of a night in which no one gave a damn about them.

As arranged, they had met at the Gare de Lyon. At the brasserie, below the Train Bleu restaurant. Dédé was sitting at a table, looking weary, a double espresso in front of him. When Rico had sat down opposite him, he had slid a handful of bills across the table.

"Your share," he had said.

It had been great to feel the money in his hand. For ten or twelve days, he had thought, he wouldn't have to beg.

His share.

Neither of them mentioned what had happened a few hours earlier. Rico did not want to think about it. It was against his deepest principles. You didn't steal. Even when things had been really bad on the street, it had never crossed his mind. But if Dédé suggested doing it again one of these days, he wasn't at all sure he'd say no. His outlook had changed. When Titi had died, he admitted, he'd gone over the edge.

In the lobby of the station, Rico had been surprised to see so many guys like him hanging around, alone or in groups. At the usual places. Tobacco shops, newspaper vendors, ticket machines . . . Rico had felt distant from them. Different. His nice parka made him look like a normal person, like any of the other travelers coming and going along the platforms.

It's incredible, he thought, how easy it is to fool people. A new parka, and you could melt into the crowd. Dressed like that, he didn't jar on anyone. As long as they didn't look at his feet, of course. Shoes always gave you away. When he was begging at the post office, he could always tell the unemployed from those who had jobs. He just had to glance at their feet.

"When I came to Paris as a student," Titi had said, "I was almost penniless for the first month. I had a garret on Rue de Luynes, on the corner of Boulevard Raspail. Every morning, I'd put on a tie and the jacket of my only suit and go out to buy bread. The woman in the bakery would make small talk with me, just the way she did with her other customers. Because of my appearance. She never imagined that once I got home I'd eat that loaf of bread on its own without anything else."

Everyone judges by appearances, whatever they say. If, right now, he went and sat down on the ground in front of the snack bar, Rico had thought, they'd immediately see him for what he was: a down-and-out. That was the way things were. And they'd start looking at him in the same old way. With pity, contempt, condescension, disgust, fear . . . Especially fear. Poverty scares people. The unemployed guys who came into the post office never looked at him, never said hello or goodbye. Most of them knew it was only a matter of time before they ended up on the street. It might happen a year, six months, a week from now. But it would happen, sooner or later.

He had walked across the lobby with the confidence of a man who has a train to catch. A place to go. His wanderings were over. He had nowhere to come back to. Nothing to hope for. Not even a glance from Julien. When the train started, these thoughts soothed him to the depths of his soul.

In spite of the parka, he felt cold all of a sudden. Cold inside. The way Titi had so often felt in those last months. Even in the sun, on their bench on Square des Batignolles.

The train was slowing down.

Rico yawned. "I think we're there,"

It was 1:55 in the morning. They were the only passengers getting off at Chalon-sur-Saône.

"Fucking one-horse town!" Dédé cursed, realizing that nothing was open in the station, and the bistros in the vicinity were closed too.

Outside, it had been snowing heavily. The first weather reports of the morning would inform the inhabitants that the temperature had dropped during the night to 12°F.

7.

WHAT'S TRUE ONE DAY CAN BE FALSE THE NEXT

Fucking one-horse town," Dédé kept muttering. He said "one-horse town" in a lingering kind of way, a real Foreign Legion way, as if it justified wiping the place off the map. That was all Chalon-sur-Saône deserved that morning. But Dédé would probably have said the same of any town in France waking up covered in snow, under a cold gray sky.

The first bar to open, the Terminus, was not especially welcoming. The owner looked at them from behind his counter as if they were mangy dogs. No hello, no smile.

"Yes?" he asked, laconically, almost without moving his lips.

"Double espresso with calvados," Rico said.

"Same for me," Dédé said. "And a slice of bread and butter."

"Yes, I'll have a slice of bread and butter too," Rico said.

The café owner's eyes went from Rico to Dédé. Without looking at him, Rico put fifty francs on the counter, and the guy served them like an automaton.

It was true they didn't look too good. After getting off the train, they had stayed on the platform, sitting on a bench sheltered by a canopy. Rico had looked around for some cartons to protect them from the cold, without finding any. Half-dozing, their backs propped against their rucksacks, they had sat and chain-smoked, waiting for a bar to open.

Now, they were advancing, silently and cautiously, along the slippery surface of Avenue du 8 Mai 1945. Chalon, still drowsy from so much snow, was slowly waking up. The snow on the sidewalks had already been trampled and was full of gray, frozen footprints.

Dédé's friend, Jo, lived in a neighborhood called La Thalie, out beyond the business area, on the northern outskirts of town. Reluctantly, the owner of the Terminus had told them how to get there.

"We should have listened to him and taken the bus," Rico moaned.

They had been walking for at least thirty minutes, and Rico was starting to get out of breath. The shooting pains in his lower back had returned. He'd have to get some Dolipran, he told himself, that always helped.

"I didn't think it was so far," Dédé said.

"A mile and a half is a mile and a half."

"Fucking one-horse town! Shit!"

Chalon, as it was revealed to them this morning, was nothing like the way Rico had imagined it. "I think it's a nice town," he had said to Dédé on the train.

At a seminar on new sales strategies, Rico had gotten friendly with a guy who worked in the region. Blandin, his name was. Or Blondin, he couldn't remember which.

"My territory's the wine route! You can imagine what that's like. Beaune, Puligny-Montrachet, Mercurey, Givry, Ruly . . . Come spend a weekend," he had suggested during another seminar. "We'll do the whole circuit. The house of wine at Chalon is worth the journey in itself. It's unique in Burgundy."

Rico had mentioned the idea to Sophie. But Burgundy wasn't one of her dream destinations. Even when he mentioned the *raviolis de grenouilles aux morilles* or the *dos de brochet aux griottes* at the Moulin de Martorey, a country restaurant highly recommended by Blandin. She preferred going to the mountains in winter, for the skiing, and to the sea—but not the Mediterranean—in summer for the sailing. She hated the countryside. It was such a peasant thing, wherever it was. And as far as wine was concerned, all that mattered was to have some in her glass. As long as it tasted O.K., she didn't care where it came from.

Rico had forgotten all about Chalon-sur-Saône and the wine route. Just as, over the years, he'd forgotten all about a lot of things he'd set his heart on. Getting a spaniel, learning to play the saxophone, walking the pilgrim road to Santiago de Compostella, visiting Petra in Jordan . . . All that mattered was Sophie. Her desires. Her happiness.

They came to a housing project. "I think this is it," Dédé muttered.

They had passed La Thalie, and had lost their way near the Chalon-North interchange. Several times, they'd had to ask for directions. Which wasn't an easy thing. They were practically the only pedestrians on this road, and most businesses were still closed.

Once they were in the project, they found Jo's place easily enough. The last block on the edge of the countryide. It was concrete, but, as Rico remarked to Dédé, it still looked a whole lot better than the outskirts of Paris.

Monique opened the door to them, a baby in her arms. Jo wasn't there. The cops had arrested him four months earlier. On a charge of murder.

"They came for him one morning," Monique said. "A whole squad of them! It's because two years ago, he was sentenced to life imprisonment in . . . What do they call it when you're not there, in court, I mean?"

"In absentia," Rico replied.

"Yes, that's it. In absentia. Sentenced to life imprisonment in absentia, for killing a guy in a squat in Aubervilliers. Jo never set foot in Aubervilliers in his life. He didn't even know where it was."

Rico remembered the case. He'd seen an item about it on TV, one evening when he was having a beer at Abdel's.

The body of Jean Marceau, known as the Belgian—a down-and-out in his sixties, a stand-up guy according to several witnesses—had been found in a squat in Aubervilliers.

Twenty-five broken ribs. He'd really taken a beating. Blows, strangulation, internal hemorrhage. The police had arrested a couple of dropouts, Rita and Ignacio, who lived on two gallons of cheap wine a day. "They admitted they'd taken part in the beating. But it was Moustache who killed the Belgian. For his monthly pension. The Belgian had just gotten it, and kept telling everyone about it."

It was the kind of thing that often happened. When you were on the street, you lost your bearings, there were no rules anymore. Only the naïve believed in the solidarity of the poor. Like many others, Rico had found that out soon enough. On the street, it was every man for himself. You could be beaten up for nothing: a sleeping bag, a nail file, a comb, a bottle of wine, a pack of cigarettes—not even a full pack—and money, especially the day when the welfare payments arrived.

How many times had Rico been beaten up since he was on the street? He couldn't remember. The last time was at Buttes-Chaumont, one afternoon in spring. He was sleeping on a bench and had felt someone's hands on him. Two young guys were searching in his pockets and even his shorts. He had struggled and the guys had started hitting him. They had taken all his money. Fortunately, Rico remembered, he'd already paid off everything he owed in various bistros. Since then, whenever he was alone, he had avoided certain places, especially stations like Châtelet, Château-Rouge, Pigalle, where he knew you were sure to be robbed.

"Moustache?" Dédé said. "You mean Moustache the Basque?"

"Yes, that's the one," Monique replied, with a grimace.

Dédé knew Moustache the Basque. He had met him in Montpellier, where he'd been bumming for a few months with Félix, a taciturn young guy who carried a football everywhere he went. Dédé had gone with the two of them to the Corbières for the grape harvest, and they'd worked together for several weeks.

"A strange guy, that Moustache. Not a bad guy, but not straight. A bigmouth too." Dédé laughed. "Worse than me. So obviously, he and I didn't get along too well."

Since the Belgian's death, Monique continued, no one had seen Moustache. But the cops had a lead. A good one. A social security card found among his things at the squat in Aubervilliers. The card was in Jo's name.

"When the cops came for Jo, they wanted him to sign a paper. 'Don't play the fool,' they told him. 'Face the facts. We have evidence it was you.' But Jo had nothing to admit. Apart from having a moustache."

"But fuck it," Dédé said, "how did his social security card end up in Moustache's pocket?"

"Well," Monique said, "one day, six months ago, Moustache turned up here with Félix in tow. A bit like the two of you, this morning. They didn't have any money. We lent them a little, and gave them clean clothes. Jo was working as a bricklayer at the time. He left early and came back late. Félix had found a job on a farm, a little way inland, with board and lodging included. But Moustache did nothing all day long. That started to piss Jo off. One day, he told Moustache he'd had enough and wanted him out. They had a really big argument."

What happened next was predictable. Moustache had taken off early in the morning after going through Jo's pockets.

"Shit!" Dédé cried. He turned to Rico. "Can you imagine that?"

Rico was gradually dozing off. It was warm in the little apartment. He had the impression the warmth was easing the pain in his back.

"Hey, you asleep?"

Rico shook his head.

"Want another beer?" Monique asked.

"If it's no bother," Dédé replied.

"How old is he?" Rico asked, pointing to the baby.

"Sixteen months. And she's a girl. Her name's Maeva."

"Can I hold her?"

The words had just slipped out. But the desire to take the child in his arms had been sudden and strong. Another life was coming back to the surface. A life he had lived. A life he had lost.

Surprised at first, Monique smiled at Rico. "Yes, all right, if you want to."

Rico rediscovered gestures he hadn't made since Julien was born. It's like swimming, he thought, you never forget how. He gently rocked Maeva, and her eyes started to close. Why, he wondered, shouldn't what's true one day also be true another day?

When they had moved to their new house in Rothéneuf, Julien had just turned two. Sophie and he were as happy as newlyweds. One morning, as he was leaving for Lorient to canvas some new customers, Rico had found a note from Sophie in his wallet. *I feel good here. The house is beautiful. I love knowing you're here, walking in the garden, looking at the sea, listening to the waves. Julien is going to be happy here, isn't he? And so are we, my love. Thank you for giving me all this happiness. I'm a lucky woman. (And you're lucky too, right?) I love you.*

Rico had never been able to make up his mind to throw away this note. He kept it, folded in four, with his identity card, and although he knew it by heart, he reread it sometimes. Just to convince himself that moments like that had really existed. That was the only reason. Because, as of today, he had given up trying to understand. And because, as Titi used to say, not all questions have answers. "They call it the mystery of life. That's all."

"And have you heard from Jo?" Dédé asked, when Monique returned with the beers.

"Well, he has his ups and downs. The guards laugh at him when he says he's innocent. In prison, they say, everyone swears they're innocent, especially the guilty. And as Jo did a few stupid things when he was young . . ."

"Fucking bastards!"

"Do you have a lawyer?" Rico asked.

Maeva had fallen asleep, but he was still rocking her gently, all the while drinking his beer.

"Oh, yes . . . A young guy, court-appointed. I certainly can't afford a lawyer on my welfare payments . . . But he seems O.K. He's been getting all the paperwork together. Wage slips, clocking-in records. To show that you can't bump off a guy in Aubervilliers at midnight and get taken on for work in Chalon at five in the morning . . ."

"And?"

"Nothing so far!" Monique said angrily. "That kind of evidence should be enough, but it isn't! He's been in the can for four months now. And the worst thing is, the fucking magistrate still hasn't questioned him. He hasn't even been brought face to face with the other two, Rita and Ignacio. Even though the lawyer says everything rests on their testimony."

Rico suddenly had a violent coughing fit. Maeva woke up and started crying. Without a word, he handed her back to Monique. He couldn't speak. He felt an overwhelming desire to spit.

"Bronchitis," he murmured, after spitting into an old Kleenex.

Bronchitis was the name he gave to whatever this illness was that was eating away at his lungs.

8.

JUST LIFE, LOVE GOING BAD FOR NO REASON

The lack of alcohol woke Rico.

He had fallen asleep on the couch, exhausted by several coughing fits. Bent double over the toilet pan, he had spat several times, then vomited. Thick, yellowish phlegm. He had come back to the living room, pale, gasping for breath, his eyes tearing up with pain.

"You O.K.?" Monique asked, worried.

"Have you got any Dolipran?"

"Just aspirin."

Rico grimaced. He didn't know what the difference was, but aspirin never brought him any relief. At the hospital, they'd given him Surbronc, to ease his cough, and Pulmicourt, an inhalant to help him breathe. They had worked. But you needed a prescription for them. Every time he asked for them, the druggists told him to go to hospital. And he didn't want to go to hospital anymore. If he set foot there, he was sure the doctors would never let him go.

"It's not serious," Rico said, collapsing on the couch. "Don't worry."

"All the same," Dédé said.

"No sweat."

He finished his glass of beer, then settled down as comfortably as he could on the couch. Gradually, the voices of Dédé and Monique faded away. Monique had resumed her story, clearly pleased to be telling tell her and Jo's misfortunes to someone.

"The guards call him Lifer," Monique was saying. "Take a shower, Lifer! Go for your walk, Lifer! Go to the canteen,

Lifer! Just to push him over the edge! Jo told the lawyer about Moustache . . . I don't mean he squealed. That wouldn't be like Jo. You know how he is . . . But he stood up for his freedom . . . And what about us, what about the kid? It's only fair, right? . . ."

The apartment was silent. Dédé, Monique and Maeva had gone. Rico extricated himself from the couch and ran to the kitchen. In search of something to drink. There were no more beers in the fridge. Or in the closet. He was starting to feel feverish. This was the thing he always dreaded, finding himself without anything to drink when he had the craving.

He finally found a bottle of Castelvin, three quarters full, under the sink. He opened it and sniffed it. It smelled sour. He lifted the neck of the plastic bottle to his lips to see if it was still drinkable or not. It was. He took a good swig of it. The liquid slipped down him like dirty water into a sewer. It was disgusting, but it was 11 proof all the same. Pleased now, he took another swig.

He'd started drinking after Sophie left. To console himself at first, to forget. Then to destroy himself. That was how he talked about it now, anyway, but at the time he didn't see things like that. He didn't analyze them. Drinking had become necessary to him. Vital. From one or two whiskies at aperitif time, he had moved on to half a bottle in the evening. One glass after another. He couldn't go to bed anymore without a strong dose of alcohol. He would stagger to the bedroom, undress and collapse on the bed. Often, he would wake up at night. About three in the morning. Then he would start over again, after having one or two glasses of water.

The fact was, he had started drinking too much that very first evening he had been on his own. Alcohol, he found, helped him to think better. To understand. He needed to understand how he and Sophie had gotten to that point. It was an obsession. But of course, there was nothing to understand. It was just life. Something two people have that goes bad one day. Like a missed appointment. Just life. Love going bad for no reason. Happiness turning to tragedy.

By mutual agreement, Sophie had moved her things out one week when Rico was away travelling in Brittany. Furniture her family had given her. Julien's brand new bedroom. Plus objects, knick-knacks she was fond of.

"Take whatever you want," he had said to her, "I don't give a damn." One evening, in a hotel room, he had imagined Sophie taking off the wall a painting by Mariano Otero, a Spanish painter who had been living in Rennes for years, and who exhibited regularly in a gallery in Dinard. They had gone there one Sunday.

The painting was called *The Kiss*. Rico had loved the sensuality of it. And the tenderness. He had given Sophie that painting for their wedding anniversary. The fifth. "I always love that moment, when our lips are half open, and quiver a little. It's just like the first time . . ." That was what he'd said, after she had unwrapped it.

"I was sure it was this! Oh, I love you!"

Sophie's warm lips had half opened, with the same emotion. And he had felt her moist, hard tongue against his. And her beautiful white breasts, swelling and eager for his hands, his caresses. And her naked body offered to him on the living room floor. They had made passionate love. Both carried away. All because of a kiss. All because of *The Kiss*.

"Can I take it?" she had asked, almost indifferently.

He had said yes. It was a gift. He was not the kind of man to take back his gifts. What did it matter, anyway? Without her kisses, this *Kiss* was meaningless now.

"And what about this?" Sophie had gone on, pointing to an old armchair they had bought in a flea market.

What about this? And this? He had said yes, and yes again. He didn't give a damn, really.

When he had returned from his rounds, he had found a note from Sophie, a fairly gentle one, waiting for him on the low table in the living room. *Don't go into the bedroom right away, or Julien's room. You'll have a shock.*

But he had immediately gone through every room. Empty or half empty. His footsteps echoed through the house. Fragments of their recent conversations came into mind. "I don't know what to tell you . . . With Alain, it's . . . as if everything's out in the open . . . Everything's simple . . . We can say anything to each other. Good things and not so good things . . . Life has stopped being a problem . . . Life is simply life . . ." Opening and closing each of the doors, it had seemed to him as if life wasn't life anymore. That it had *simply* left. And silence and death had taken its place.

That evening, he made himself spaghetti with butter, and ate it standing up. Listening to old Charles Aznavour songs.

Love is like a day
It ends, it goes away . . .

Songs to cry to, for when you want to cry. Rico had always liked Aznavour because of that. Because tears were so near the surface.

Love is sun and feasts, love is moon and quarrels
Love is rain and battles . . .

Holding his plate, he walked from one room to another, reopening the doors, switching on all the lights. Every time he went back in the living room, he had a large glass of red wine. Saint-Émilion. A Château-Robin 1997. He and Éric had brought back some bottles from a bachelor jaunt in the Bordeaux region.

Rico finished the bottle then, collapsing into an armchair, started on the whisky. Aznavour was singing "To Die of Love." On a forty-track compilation. Enough to get him through the evening. Later, totally drunk, he slipped naked between the sheets and jerked off, weeping and thinking of Sophie. He sobbed as he came. And the sobs stayed with him all through the night.

That was how he spent the first week. Drowning himself in alcohol every evening. Jerking off too. His head full of fragments of things Sophie had said. "It hurts me to know I've hurt you. It hurts me to see you hurt . . . It's like a weight inside me. I live with it, but it never goes away . . ." Bullshit! he would scream. Bullshit! "I'd like to see you happy, one day soon. I'd like to see you smile again . . . You deserve love, tenderness, happiness . . ."

Bullshit! Words, words, as Dalida used to sing. Hot air! Words you say and then forget as soon as you're in someone else's arms. In someone else's bed, and his swollen cock enters you and thrusts deep into you . . . Sophie being fucked by Alain. The images were impossible to get rid of, and they made him refill his glass. One last drink and then he'd sleep . . . But every evening, he needed one more drink.

Sophie! he would cry, panting. Sophie, he would weep. And he would keep jerking off. Until his cock, red and sore, burned his fingers.

He would jerk off until he couldn't come anymore.

Sophie.

Until he couldn't love anymore.

By the time the weekend had come and gone, he realized that no one had called him. None of his friends. Not even Éric. All of them, especially Éric, were on Sophie and Alain's side. Rico was the loser of the couple, and other couples don't like losers.

Much later, one noon when they met to discuss the divorce, Sophie told Rico that everything had started between her and Alain at a lunch party organized by Annie. One Sunday, one of those Sundays when he was in Paris attending yet another course for the sales force, she had invited a few people over. Her sister Isa, Isa's husband Claude, Sophie, and Alain.

"That really shocked me, you know," Sophie had said.

She meant it. And he believed her.

"And I said so to Annie, in the kitchen."

"Don't make such a fuss," Annie had replied. "I bet your man"—Annie always called him that, putting as much contempt into the word "man" as the conventions allowed—"has the occasional fling with one of his female colleagues."

"Maybe. I don't know."

"All those conferences, all those courses he goes on . . . You know what men are like . . . Believe me, it's best to keep them where you can see them."

They had both laughed. And Annie had said, conspiratorially, "Shall I put you opposite each other, or side by side?"

Annie probably hadn't imagined that this lunch would turn Sophie's life upside down. Or that it would destroy their marriage. She had probably assumed that Sophie and Alain would sleep together, might even have an affair. She hated Rico so much, she certainly had no objection to the idea.

When Sophie told him she had met "someone else," Rico knew immediately she was talking about Alain. Who else could it be? He'd noticed how Alain hovered around her. Whether meeting at someone's house or during their ski trips. It even amused Rico to catch Alain eyeing Sophie's ass, or staring at her legs when she crossed or uncrossed them. "Yes, she's beautiful, my friend," he would think, "but she's mine, all mine."

All his. He believed that. But nothing's ever fixed. Nothing can ever be taken for granted. He should have known that, after all the songs he'd listened to on the car radio! Maybe if he had been a little less sure of himself, or a little more jealous, he would have realized that Sophie wasn't indifferent to Alain's glances, Alain's desire for her.

There was only one time when Rico had gotten a little worried.

Alain, who prided himself on being a good photographer, had invited all of them to his place to show them the slides of their last skiing trip. The kind of ritual occasion Rico found particularly boring and stupid. That day, though, he didn't doze off as soon as the first images were projected. Even though Sophie wasn't always in the foreground, she was in almost all the photos.

The last slide came on the screen. Sophie had taken this one. Alain was sitting on his ass in the snow, his legs spread wide. Between his legs, carved in the snow, an erect penis and two nice round testicles. Alain was looking at the camera and smiling, with the tip of his tongue protruding slightly. Everyone had burst out laughing. Sophie more than anyone else.

"Would you like to suck his dick?" he asked her as soon as they got home.

"You're so vulgar. It was just a joke."

"Me, vulgar? It'd never have occurred to me to do something like that. Let alone have my photograph taken by a friend's wife."

"You're a killjoy. You see the bad in everything."

"I see what I see," Rico said, raising his voice a little, unusually for him. "That he's showing his dick. That's what I see. Which makes me wonder if you'd like to suck it."

"Ah . . . so monsieur is jealous, is he?" she replied, sarcastically. "No one can do anything, with you around. We can't amuse ourselves, we can't even laugh. You always have to look for . . . I don't know what . . . a meaning where there isn't one.

Annie and Isa were there, and yes, we laughed a lot. If you had even a tiny sense of humor, it could have been you making us laugh . . ."

"Now that's an idea. Next time, I'll show them my ass!"

Sophie left the room to go to bed, but without slamming the door as she sometimes did. When he joined her in bed, she was leafing through a women's magazine. A special dieting issue. He glanced over her shoulder.

"Are you interested in this?"

"I'm only interested in you," he replied gently.

"I know that," she said with a smile. "Shall I switch off?" And as she said it, she did so.

He put his arms around her. "I'm sorry about earlier," he whispered in her ear.

He didn't mean it. But he wanted to fuck her. Just to get his revenge on Alain. His cock in the snow. The way he made Sophie laugh. His desire for her. That was the only reason. And to reassure himself too. To convince himself that he was still the love of her life. And that his own cock was irreplaceable.

"I'm sorry," he said again, this time sliding his hand inside her pajama top.

"It's late . . ."

"Do you think so?"

And he put his erect cock against her naked buttocks. Sophie parted her thighs for him to caress her the way she liked. But Rico entered her suddenly and violently.

"Oh!" she cried out. "It's huge."

He lifted her to take her doggie-fashion. And for the first time in his life, he made love to Sophie without any love at all, without any tenderness. He fucked her for himself. Forcefully. As if marking out his territory.

After Sophie left, Rico often wondered if that night, and the nights that followed, she had thought about Alain when he fucked her.

He supplied his own answer. Yes.

"Fucking bitch," he said, putting the bottle back on the sink.

"I don't care. I have my ball."

For some minutes, Félix had been watching Rico.

9.

LIZARD'S HEAD, LIZARD'S TAIL

Félix gave Rico a big smile. A shy, profoundly sad—and unsettling—smile.

"My name's Félix."

Absorbed in his own thoughts, Rico had not heard him come in, and he had jumped when he saw him standing there, a slender, motionless, silent figure. It was if he had been listening to all the things Rico had been saying to himself in his head.

This had to be Félix, Rico knew that. Jo and Dédé's friend. Because of the football he was holding under his arm. But Rico had been surprised all the same. It had never occurred to him that Félix was still around. Dédé and Monique hadn't mentioned it, at least before he fell asleep.

Félix was hopping from one foot to another, as if he was desperate to take a leak.

"How did you get in?" Rico asked.

"Coming and going's not a problem."

Rico could not take his eyes of this shaggy-haired figure wriggling in front of him. Especially the tattoo at the corner of Félix's left eye. A lizard's head.

"Lizard's head," Félix said.

He shifted the ball from his left arm to his right arm, then opened his left hand and showed Rico his palm. The lizard's tail.

"Lizard's tail," Félix said with a laugh.

They looked at each other in silence. Félix stopped hopping, then declared in a monotonous voice, "Monique and Dédé went to the supermarket. To do the shopping. There's nothing in the fridge."

"Want some?" Rico said finally, holding out the bottle to Félix.

He grimaced and shook his head. "I have my ball."

Rico nodded, as if to say he understood. Then he took another long swig, looked at what was left in the bottle and decided to finish it. If they'd gone to the supermarket, they'd bring back some wine, for sure. Dédé wouldn't forget.

"Do you live here?" Rico asked, following Félix into the living room.

"No," he replied, sitting down on the couch. "In the forest. I have a cabin."

"You live in a cabin? In this weather?"

"I can't sleep in houses. Houses stink at night."

Rico didn't reply. Again, he was mesmerized by that lizard's head bursting from the corner of Félix's left eye. He wondered if the lizard's tail moved when Félix blinked.

"Haven't you noticed? Houses stink at night. There's this kind of smell, as soon as you close your eyes. A smell of pu-tre-fac-tion," he said, separating each syllable, as if he had just discovered the word.

Rico shrugged. He didn't know anything about that. He'd forgotten what it was like to live in a house. This apartment was different. It was like being between two worlds. And he wouldn't be staying.

"I can't breathe it. Before, I never even noticed . . ."

Félix broke off, smiled at Rico, then grabbed the remote control and switched on the TV.

"They show lots of cartoons on Wednesdays. I like cartoons. That's why I came."

He channel-hopped until something caught his attention.

"The Power Rangers! Hey, I love that show!"

He settled on the couch, his ball held tight against his chest, and didn't say another word, spellbound by the images on the screen.

Some time during the afternoon, Dédé had told Rico that no one knew where Félix came from. Moustache had met him one day in Toulouse, at a reception center run by Abbé Pierre called the Casa. At night, he slept next to the prefabricated huts that were used as dormitories. Everyone assumed he was crazy. One night, as a joke, Moustache had suggested they travel together. Félix had stuck with Moustache. Until Moustache took off, without warning, after his argument with Jo.

At that time, Dédé had continued, Félix never spoke. He could only say two sentences: "I'm alone" and "I have my ball." And he would repeat them, until it drove everyone crazy. According to Abdul, one of the people in charge of the Casa, Félix had ended up on the street after a long stay in a mental hospital. Before that, he had worked on a small farm. Which explained why he liked nature so much.

It was while kicking a ball with Abdul for fifteen minutes each day that Félix had started talking again. A little. But without ever really opening up about himself.

"He doesn't remember anything," Dédé had said. "Just fragments. He remembers he grew up in a state orphanage. And that he used to have a wife and child. But it was all 'a long time ago.' He has no idea how long he's been on the street. It's like he doesn't have any notion of time."

"What about his tattoos?"

"He's had those done since he's been on the street. But God alone knows where! And anyway, if you ask him too many questions, he always answers that he'd 'rather not talk about it' . . ."

"I don't like the commercials," Félix said.

And he started channel hopping again. Then he turned to Rico and smiled. "A ball is better than a dog. It's more faithful. More faithful even than a woman. Did your wife leave too?"

Rico nodded.

"I'm alone too. But it's O.K. now, I have my ball."

"Yes, so I see."

Another cartoon came on and Félix became so absorbed in it, he seemed to forget Rico was even there.

Rico was feeling feverish again. The cheap wine he had drunk hadn't had the desired effect. He was still thirsty. For a moment, he thought he might join Monique and Dédé at the supermarket, but then he thought about all that snow outside, and the cold, and decided against it. What was the point, he thought, they wouldn't be much longer.

Rico had tried to stop drinking once. A few months after meeting Titi. At the time—the end of his first year on the street—he was drinking forty cans of beer a day. Kronenbourg or Bavaria, whichever he could afford. His day was divided into blocks of four or five hours. Time enough for sleep, then another dose. And this would happen three or four times a day.

"Drop the beer, and start drinking wine," Titi advised him. "And try to keep to about a gallon. A gallon is my dose. Don't go beyond that, or you're fucked. It's the slippery slope."

Rico agreed, of course. He already knew all about alcohol and its effects. The total lack of reflexes. The permanent feeling of pins and needles in the legs. The loss of balance. Already toward the end of his time with Malika, he kept hurting himself on the stairs. Even at night, when he got up to take a leak, he often fell.

"Yes, you're right," he had replied to Titi.

But he couldn't control himself. On the contrary. He'd started drinking wine—Bienvenu and Fleurval—but had continued with beer too.

"How much have you drunk since this morning?" Titi asked.

They had decided to walk to Sacré-Coeur, and on the steps of the Butte Montmartre, Rico started to drag his feet. He was tired and out of breath.

"Stop pissing me off, Titi! Who do you think you are, Jiminy Cricket? Just leave me alone, will you!"

Rico collapsed onto a step. Determined not to move. Ready to die on the spot. In any case, he didn't have any strength left. His legs wouldn't carry him anymore.

"Go ahead, then! Die, asshole!" Titi climbed a few more steps, then turned and said, "I'll piss on you when I see you in the gutter . . ."

Rico lit a cigarette. He took two drags, nervously, then started crying, like a kid caught doing something he shouldn't. Without his noticing, Titi had come back and sat down next to him.

"For fuck's sake, don't start bawling!"

"I'll stop, Titi. I'll stop drinking. Tomorrow."

That was when Titi tried to tell him that he couldn't do it alone. He needed medical help. The best thing was to go to hospital. He'd go with him tomorrow.

But of course, Rico wouldn't listen. He told himself he could manage. And he could do it on his own, like a grown-up. Just to prove to himself that he was still capable of taking control of his life. All the next day, and the days that followed, he avoided going anywhere where he could run into Titi.

He'd held out for three days. Three days of hell. He almost went crazy. On the second day, he started sweating, then shaking. He drank gallons of water. He had heard that alcohol dehydrated you and you needed to drink lots of water.

It was at noon on the third day that the "accident" happened. He was walking along Rue Alexandre-Dumas. His hands suddenly went all tense, and he couldn't untangle his fingers. Then his whole body froze. His eyes misted over. His legs gave way. And he collapsed. A woman cried out, "My God!" He remembered that. And the strident blast of a car horn, because his body had rolled out onto the road.

When he came to, he was in hospital. The doctors gave him a talking-to. They said pretty much what Titi had said.

Wanting to stop drinking was a laudable aim. But it wasn't easy. You needed help. Aftercare. "Especially with a cirrhotic liver like yours," the doctor said. He explained to Rico that the lack of Vitamin B in his diet increased the toxicity of the alcohol. He would have to be given vitamin injections. Ten injections a month, for two months.

In the five days he spent in hospital, Rico's spirits improved. He was fed, housed, looked after. Everything became simple again. Life. The future. Once he was cured, he'd make a fresh start. He'd finally recover.

Recovery. That was the word that was always in his mind. It was like a magic potion. He'd talk about it with the nurses, when they took the time to listen to him. "Getting real work straight away is too much to ask, I know. But there are lots of little jobs, aren't there? Messenger, delivery man, window cleaner. Just to help me recover."

The first week, he went for all his injections. Every other day. Then his visits became less frequent. One morning, he decided not to go back. Surviving on the street took all his energy. The time he spent in hospital, the time it took to get there and come back, was time he could spend begging. With only forty or fifty francs in his pocket in the evening, life was getting hard again.

"Why don't they give us a bit of money during the treatment?"

"It's a hospital," Titi replied. "A hospital, not a charity."

Titi meant it humorously, but Rico didn't laugh.

With Titi's help, he negotiated his relationship with alcohol. He drank, but he drank sensibly. In order never to be caught short. He took Titi's advice and forced himself to always buy his wine at the same grocery, drink his beer in the same bar.

"They're markers," he had said. "If you see the same face too many times in a day, you'll know you're over the limit."

Rico graduated to a gallon of wine and ten beers a day.

That lasted for a year. But gradually, he deviated from this routine. He allowed himself "extras." Spirits. Vodka, whisky. At night at first, then at the end of the day. Especially in the last few months. And Titi's death didn't help.

He sensed the lizard's head on him. Félix was looking at him. The same way he'd looked at him in the kitchen. Rico noticed that his hands were moist. Mechanically, he wiped them on his jeans.

"You want me to get you some wine?" Félix asked.

"Where from?"

"One of the neighbors. A retired guy. He always keeps a stock, and he knows me. Shall I get you a bottle?"

Rico gave Félix fifty francs, and Félix went off to see the neighbour, still holding his ball. He brought back a bottle of Valombre. One step above Castelvin. The bottle was even made of glass.

"Here," Félix said, giving him his change. "He charged me fifteen francs. It's expensive, but he's a poor old guy, so you can't blame him. And he's always there, in case . . ."

Rico's hands shook as he unscrewed the top of the bottle. Félix grabbed it and filled him a glass. Rico drank it slowly, then poured himself another, which he didn't touch. Now that he had a fifth of a gallon of wine within reach, he felt calmer.

"For me, it's the smell," Félix said. "I can't stand it. Wine, beer, anything."

"Didn't you ever drink?"

"Before, I think. Like everyone else. But now . . ."

"Now you have your ball."

"That's right. It's really important. We'll go kick it around a little later on. I'm good, you'll see."

"Maybe."

"Yes, later. When they're back. There's no hurry, is there?"

Rico was starting to like Félix. He was like a teenager. In the way he moved, the way he talked. With great fragility and, at the same time, great confidence. What had surprised Rico, earlier, in the kitchen, was the look in Félix's eyes. As if he wasn't sure where he was, maybe even who he was. The lizard's head somehow emphasized this feeling.

What would happen, Rico wondered, if someone tried to take away his ball? Would he turn violent? Or would he say nothing and just go off into a corner somewhere to die? But what difference did it make? It wouldn't change what Félix was.

"What's on TV?"

"Don't know," Félix replied, pleased that someone was sharing his enthusiasm. "Shall we switch channels?"

A real kid, Rico said to himself again. He drank some of his wine, settled comfortably on the couch. He felt the back of Félix's neck resting on his shoulder. The lizard's head turned to him. There was something soothing about it. Everything was fine now. An episode of *Inspector Gadget* was starting.

"Perfect!" Félix cried. "This is the life, eh?"

It was the only life left, Rico thought.

10.

MEANINGLESS MOMENTS,
STOLEN FROM TIME AS IT PASSES

That night, Rico slept on the couch. He didn't sleep well. He kept tossing and turning, trying to find a comfortable position so that he could get to sleep.

On the other side of the living room wall, Maeva would moan from time to time, and he would hear Monique whispering "Shh, shh . . ." to calm her. After a while, Maeva started crying and Monique got up. She came out of the bedroom carrying the little girl, crossed the living room and went into the kitchen.

"Shhh . . . Shhh. There, there, sweetheart, there, there . . . It's over . . . Come, now . . . Shhh . . ."

Rico assumed that, since Jo's arrest, Monique had been letting Maeva sleep in her bed. The warmth of another body must have been a comfort for both of them. But that night, Dédé had taken Maeva's place in the bed. Her father's place. And that must have been what was upsetting the little girl.

During the evening—they were on their sixth or seventh Ricard, but who was keeping count?—Dédé had leaned toward Rico and whispered, "Hot, isn't she?"

He nodded toward the kitchen, where Monique was making spaghetti Bolognese. It wasn't a question. Just the easiest way to tell Rico that the two of them were going to sleep together that night. And that he, Rico, had to understand. If you had the opportunity to get laid, you'd be a fool to pass it up.

Yes, Rico could understand that. He'd only gotten laid twice since he'd been on the street. The first time was with Monika, a German girl who bummed around Edgar-Quinet. He'd bought her a beer and a sandwich at the Café d'Odessa, then fucked her in a coin-operated toilet. The second time was with a hooker on Rue du Caire, to celebrate his first year as a bum. Three hundred francs, it had cost him. A fortune.

"You're in, and then you're out, and it's over," Dédé had said one evening when Rico was with the gang, eyeing women in the metro. "And you never get your money back. Eh, Titi?"

"I prefer to use my eyes rather than my dick. It's cheaper that way. Besides, for me to get a hard-on I'd need . . . I don't know, Claudia Schiffer!"

"Get a load of that one!" Fred had said.

A little brunette, with an ass that was too big for her tight-fitting jeans, had just passed them.

"She's just a big lump, bozo!" Lulu had replied.

"Who cares? I could fuck her . . ."

"And how do you manage?" Rico had asked Dédé.

"If I pick up a woman, I take her to a hotel. I like fucking in a bed."

Titi, who was starting to get drunk, had sung:

. . . going home with your heart shot to hell
and your dick in your hand . . .

Rico had shrugged. So Monique was hot, was she? Well, why not? Although the idea of taking her in his arms didn't exactly give him a hard-on. Far from it. Nothing about her aroused his desire. She had the tired, flaccid, prematurely aged body of one of those women life hasn't been kind to. Women on welfare, divorcées, battered wives . . . He'd seen plenty of them at the post office on Rue des Boulets. Even the ones who made an effort to disguise the lines on their faces and the bags under their eyes with make-up were instantly recognizable. By the weary way they moved. By their hesitant gestures, which gave away the fact that they were on tranquilizers.

They were all hot, these women. Like Monique. But their

hopes of finding a man for sex dwindled a little more every day. Like their hopes of finding work, or a better paid job if they were already in work. So they clung on to whatever lifelines they could find, however tenuous. Their children. The kindness of a clerk at the unemployment office. A lecherous wink from the head of their department. Even a greeting from a down-and-out at the entrance to the post office. Until the opportunity presented itself. A man, any man. Moments of victory over the long, sad, lonely nights. Moments stolen from time as it passed. Meaningless moments.

"She's your friend's wife," was all Rico had said in reply.

"True. But the thing is, we don't know how long that idiot Jo is going to be inside for. Maybe life, as they say. You know what the fucking law is like . . . And anyway," he added with a smile, "she hasn't had anything to get her teeth into for four months now!"

"You don't think Félix . . . she and Félix . . ."

"She'd have told me."

Rico hadn't insisted. Things had happened that day that he was only just becoming aware of.

Dédé and Monique had come back just after noon from their trip to the supermarket.

"Fucking one-horse town!" Dédé had cried, as he came in. "Finding a bar open in this town takes forever!"

Dédé and Monique had had a few beers on their way home. Just to buck themselves up before facing the cold again.

"We're better off in here," Monique had said with a laugh, opening the shopping bags.

Ham, sausage and cheese for lunch. Pasta, ground meat and tomato sauce for dinner. Plus a bottle of Ricard, a twelve-pack of beers and six bottles of wine, which they had stuffed into Maeva's stroller.

"I got a good one," Dédé had proclaimed, showing him a bottle. "Corbières."

Domaine du Capitoul, the label said. It smelled good: a hint of the South. But there was no comparison with a good Burgundy from the Côte Chalonnaise or the Côte de Beaune. Mercurey, Rully, Pommard, Volnay or Corton. The wines his friend Blandin had talked about.

During his sleepless night, Rico thought again about the trip to Burgundy he had given up on. About all the things he hadn't done in his life. All the things he hadn't experienced. All the things that were now out of reach. Huddled on the couch, with a thick blanket over him, he was like an old man on his deathbed, drawing up a balance sheet of his life.

The image of his mother dying in hospital came back to him. The memory of her pale, tearful eyes. Eyes that at last admitted how wrong she'd been to accept everything, endure everything, being in every way—her tastes, her opinions, even the way she dressed—a mere shadow of her husband. His father Raymond, who, barely six months after the funeral, had gotten married again, to a young cousin of his mother's named Marie-Laure.

"So what?" he had said, trying to justify himself. "I'm still young."

"That's not what I'm blaming you for, you know that."

"If your mother hadn't been sick, Marie-Laure and me . . . We've been seeing each other for more than five years . . . I love her, can't you understand that?"

Rico didn't reply. Marie-Laure was his latest conquest, but she certainly wasn't the first. He couldn't forget the way his mother had cried her eyes out, some evenings when Raymond hadn't come home.

Rico's silence embarrassed his father. He sighed, then continued, "I don't have anything to be ashamed of. I stayed with your mother to the end, without fail!"

"And every night, without fail, you fucked Marie-Laure! Isn't that it?"

"You have no right to talk to me like that!"

All the things that had rankled with Rico for years were coming to a boil. His father's selfishness. His smugness. The way he controlled other people's lives. The way he decided what was good for him and bad for them.

"Mother gave you everything. She always gave you everything. Just so *you* could succeed. Just so *you* could climb the fucking career ladder . . . You never gave her the chance to be . . . herself."

"Herself . . ." Raymond echoed, shaking his head wearily. "Her head was full of dreams out of trashy magazines. All that crap she used to read . . . I'll tell you this, and I'm sorry if it shocks you, but I only put up with your mother because of you . . ."

"Go on, say it! You sacrificed yourself for me, is that it?"

During his military service, in Djibouti, Rico had sent Raymond a letter. Telling him he'd always been a selfish bastard. "I kill myself for the two of you." That was what he always said. "For the two of you." But he'd never heard him say, "I love the two of you." And he'd never said to him, "I love you."

"Go fuck yourself!" Rico had cried.

They hadn't seen each other for years. Or written. Or phoned. They'd sent him a card when Julien was born, but that had been Sophie's idea. Even when he'd started to go downhill, Rico hadn't turned to him. He was still too full of disgust for the man, and too ashamed of himself. It was only after six months of wandering and humiliation on the street that he had resigned himself and gone to Saint-Brieuc to see his father, as a last resort.

He waited for him outside his office. The man who came quickly toward him seemed like a stranger. Or maybe it was the other way around. This man was still his father, but Rico wasn't his son anymore. Instead of embracing him, his father held out his hand and Rico found himself shaking it, as if it were a stranger's hand.

"The thing you asked me over the phone," Raymond began. "It isn't possible."

They were sitting at a table at the Taverne du Chapeau-Rouge, near the cathedral.

"I can't lay my hands on fifty thousand francs, and I can't borrow it. Marie-Laure and I have just bought a house in Auray. An old fisherman's cottage. It needs a lot of work done on it . . ."

Rico thought about his mother's grave. He had gone to the cemetery before meeting his father, and had found the grave neglected, without flowers. He had felt a pang in his heart, seeing that gray tombstone with nothing on it, just the inscription: *My beloved wife . . . My dearest mother . . .* It had seemed to him even more squalid than death. Suffering and death. Sadness and death. He had gone back to town and bought a bunch of daisies with the little money he had in his pocket.

"I dropped by the cemetery," he said with mounting anger. All his old resentment had returned.

"I haven't had time to take care of it," his father replied.

They looked at each other. Defiantly.

"What are you going to do now?" Raymond asked, finishing his beer.

Rico stood up. "Do you really care?"

His father made no attempt to stop him. He didn't suggest he should come to the house and spend the evening with them, stay the night, stay a few days. They didn't even shake hands.

Everyone has his own life to live, Rico muttered, lighting a cigarette. As he smoked, he wondered if, when you came down to it, that was what life was: each person trying to hold on to what he has and survive in the middle of so much human stupidity . . . Maybe his father was right. Maybe Sophie was right. Wasn't he the proof of that? He had gone under, whereas for them, everything had continued. Life. Love. Happiness.

No, he thought, throwing back the blanket, that couldn't be it. But what, then? What exactly had he done wrong? Not only him, but Dédé, Monique, Jo. And Félix. And what about guys like Titi, smart guys who'd read lots of books? If guys like Titi went under, it meant that something, somewhere, wasn't right. But what, dammit?

He remembered a song Titi liked to sing. It was an old song, and he couldn't remember either the title or the name of the singer.

It's fake, it's phony, it's a sham
It's bogus, it's tinsel, it's a con
It's trash, it's froth, it's a trick
It's love, first it's there, now it's gone

Love that's gone. That was it. Everywhere you looked. Between a husband and a wife. A father and his son. A brother and a sister. Two friends . . . And doors that close. Until, one day, the last one closes. The last door before hell.

Hell was the street. Hell was poverty.

How many like him were there, wandering the streets? Tramping the roads of France? No one bothered to count them anymore. Hundreds, it was said. Thousands. They only counted the dead these days, and then only in winter.

"I think I might stay here a while," Dédé had said, confidentially. "With her."

"O.K., but I'm leaving. Tomorrow, probably. I still want to get to Marseilles."

"There's no rush, you know."

"I know."

They had poured themselves another round of Ricard, and Dédé, as if instinctively rediscovering the gestures of a lover, had stood up and gone to the kitchen to take Monique her drink. Rico had heard them clinking glasses, kissing, laughing.

When Dédé had come back, he had said, again in a confidential tone, "You know, I listened to you the other night. You have to get that woman out of your mind. That Sophie."

"Why are you telling me that?"

"Because that bitch ate your heart and spat it out. And now she's doing the same to your head. She's not worth it, in my opinion."

Rico was surprised to hear Dédé talk like that.

"I tell you what she deserves . . . To get reamed by a stranger on a street corner."

Rico had smiled at the idea. "What difference would that make?"

Dédé had shrugged. "How the hell should I know? That's for you to say."

"The pasta's ready!" Monique had called from the kitchen.

Then she had joined them in the living room, with her glass in her hand. "Where's Félix?"

"He was here a while ago," Dédé replied. He turned to Rico. "Did you see him go?"

Rico did not reply. He remembered what Félix had told him that morning, "Coming and going's no problem." Félix was as silent and discreet as a shadow. Or a ghost. Their ghost.

Rico had finished his cigarette. He stubbed it out, then poured himself a glass of wine. He filled it to the brim, without shaking. And drank it to the last drop. With his eyes closed. Sophie was naked in front of him. She was dancing, writhing. Arching her back. Offering him her lovely ass. He really wanted to strangle her, just as he had in his nightmare.

11.

THE SUN, THE SUN . . . BUT ALSO REGRET

Outside, it was still dark. In the kitchen, Rico drank two large glasses of water, then started making coffee. He grabbed the bottle of Ricard and half filled the glass. He knocked it back, just like that, neat. The taste of the anis made him shudder. He grimaced, then poured himself another, smaller shot, which he drank after lighting a cigarette.

There was no way he was going back to sleep now. He wasn't sure he'd slept at all, maybe he'd only dozed a little. But he didn't feel tired. He hadn't had any more coughing fits, at least none as violent as that morning, and his back pain seemed to have subsided. "It's the country air," Félix had said, when they had gone down to the parking lot in the afternoon. "Towns kill you."

They had kicked the ball around in the snow. Félix was a real expert. He used his feet, his knees, his chest, his head. Rico had rediscovered a simple pleasure he hadn't known since he was a child. Kicking a can. Dribbling with a big stone. Kicking a real ball. Soccer was another thing he'd given up. His father had never liked him to play. Not even in the high school team. It was too common, and it meant he'd mix with bad company. As a result, he had given up all sports. His father thought there was a kind of unhealthy machismo in sport. Instead, he'd enrolled him in the Boy Scouts. The children there were from respectable families, and they were taught how to function as a community. Starting with his first summer camp, Rico was initiated into forbidden pleasures. Timid caresses. Furtive kisses. Masturbation. It was the origin of his lifelong disgust with religion.

"I'm good, aren't I?" Félix kept saying, hopping from one foot to the another, as happy as a kid.

"Have you ever played soccer? In a team?"

"Amateur."

"You played as an amateur?"

"No, I'm an amateur. I watch matches on TV."

It wasn't impossible to have a conversation with Félix, but what he said wasn't very coherent. Often, after two or three sentences—as Dédé had warned him—he'd bring the discussion to a close with the words "I'd rather not talk about it."

"I used to have a Vespa. A real one. My wife and I set off one day to ride all over France."

"And how was it?"

"She didn't like the Vespa. Or camping. So you see, I'd rather not talk about it."

"I understand."

"How about you?"

"I never had a Vespa!"

Félix had burst out laughing. He seemed pleased. "Go on! Go on, shoot!" he had cried, throwing the ball again.

Next, Félix had decided he wanted to show him his cabin.

They had walked for at least fifteen minutes, past snow-covered fields. On the way there, the only footprints were those that Félix had left that morning. Several times, he had turned to Rico to make sure he was all right. And every time, Rico had thought he saw the lizard's head smiling at the corner of Félix's eye.

The cabin was a garden shed. At the edge of a grove of trees.

"Good, isn't it?"

Inside, a camp bed and a large sleeping bag. On a crate, a camp stove, an Italian coffee maker and an iron cup. A jerry can full of water in a corner. And pinned up on a wall, a photo of Sophie Marceau, topless.

"My wife," Félix had said, with a hint of admiration. Then

he laughed. "Well, not her . . . My wife always wanted to look like her. Ever since high school . . ."

He had waited for a question from Rico. But all Rico had said was, "She has beautiful breasts"—adding in a slightly mocking tone, "But I guess you'd rather not talk about it."

Félix had smiled. "That's right. Best not to talk about it." Instead, he'd started talking about the farmer he worked for. He was a young guy, he had said. Like him. He'd been a bum too before settling here.

"His name's Norbert. He was on the road for years . . . Driving a motor bike. An old one. He still has it. He sometimes lends it to me . . . but only to drive in the country."

The farm was a few minutes from the cabin. It was quite small.

"Hey, you're not going to believe this, but he met his wife, Anne, at a soup kitchen! She was a voluntary worker . . . She's cute, Anne," he had added, thoughtfully. "Not quite like Sophie Marceau, but . . ."

"And is his farm doing O.K.?"

"Norbert told me he's a hundred and fifty thousand francs in debt. Crazy, isn't it? The tractor, the van . . . I'd be scared. Wouldn't you?"

Rico thought about the money he had borrowed. About the day he had signed the contract of their house in Rothéneuf. A million and a half. All their savings had gone into it. And thirty years to pay it off. It had all gone up in smoke. Nothing but ashes now. Lost forever. A dream that had died.

"As long as they're happy," he had replied.

Félix had nodded in agreement. "I don't suppose you have time to find out, when you're working hard. But they're nice . . ."

Félix stared out over the snowy landscape. The lizard's head squinted at the farm. At that simple life that might be happiness. Two people who love each other. Smoke rose from the chimney of the old farmhouse, as if in a child's drawing. Love, loving each other, was the only thing worth betting on.

"Aren't you cold?" Félix had asked him on the way back.

The sky had become overcast, and it had started to snow again. Rico had come to a halt, and stood there, lost in thought, remembering the first time he had seen snow, as a child. Standing at the edge of a field. The flakes falling faster and faster, thicker and thicker, onto the palm of his outstretched hand. He had laughed. He had roared with laughter.

"No," Rico had replied. "No, it won't always be cold."

Rico poured himself another cup of coffee, and lit another cigarette. The night seemed endless. He wished Titi were around, to tell him stories. Titi loved telling stories. Things he had lived through. Novels he had read.

He did that sometimes, when they were on their bench on Square des Batignolles, and they couldn't think of anything to say to each other. When the silence between them was too heavy while life went on around them. Mothers chattering away and smiling. Children running, shouting, laughing, crying. Pieces of dry bread being thrown to the ducks, down on the pond. Teenagers, mostly high school kids cutting classes, lying under the trees, kissing greedily, shamelessly. The old man with the mane of white hair waiting patiently for his wife who would never return . . .

Titi had talked about *Lord Jim* by Conrad, *The Trembling of a Leaf* by Somerset Maugham, *The Power and the Glory* by Graham Greene. Rico had never been sure if these were real novels, or just stories that Titi made up as he went along. So he had been surprised one day when Titi had started telling the story of *Treasure Island*.

"I've read that one! When I was a boy. Who did you say it was by?"

"Robert Louis Stevenson. My favorite."

"Go on, tell me about it!"

But Titi wasn't here anymore. And the stories that kept going through Rico's head, the stories he would tell himself, were his own. He knew it was time to let everything back in. It didn't matter now. He was at the end of his tether, and the only person to blame was himself. Not Sophie. Not Malika. Not even Julie.

Julie.

It was when he met her that life had really gone off the rails. For good. One night.

He'd felt stifled, all alone in that huge, empty house. So he had set off for Rennes, to see a movie. There was a new Clint Eastwood picture playing. As he drove, he was really looking forward to it. But once he'd parked his car, on Quai Lamennais, not far from the movie theater, he hesitated. Suddenly afraid of running into Sophie and Alain. Or Éric and Annie. Or all four of them. Or someone else he knew. Afraid of letting them see him as he was, a man alone. Lonely and adrift.

So he had climbed the few steps leading to Rue Montfort and gone into the Chatham, a bar that stayed open until late. They served really good whisky there. It was packed, as usual. He squeezed his way to the end of the bar counter and made some space for himself. Just enough so that the barman noticed him. He ordered an Oban, without ice. Julie was sitting on a stool next to him, an empty glass in front of her. She looked as if she was waiting for someone who was clearly not going to show up.

She glanced at him. Dark eyes, like Léa's. Rico could only say that now, having come to Marseilles because of his memories of Léa. But he hadn't thought of her at the time. He had forgotten Léa. Or rather, he'd buried her so deep inside his head that he thought he had forgotten her. He'd once wondered aloud, "You know, maybe when you get down to it, I was always unfaithful to Sophie. That's why it all went wrong in the end . . ." As usual, I hadn't known what to answer.

Rico felt an immediate desire for this woman.

"Are you waiting for someone?"

The music was deafening. You had to raise your voice to make yourself heard.

"No," she shouted. "How about you?"

He laughed. "No one's waiting for me."

"I see," she said, with a smile.

"Can I buy you a drink?"

"Sure." She leaned toward him and said in his ear, "Drinking's my favourite game. I hold the record."

Her voice was already thick with alcohol, but Rico didn't notice. He was too busy looking Julie over from head to foot. A cute little thing, he thought. And for the first time since Sophie had left, he imagined himself in bed with a woman, this woman. Deep in her eyes, there was something he had recognized. An attraction. He hadn't realized that it was nothing but an immense weariness with life. His sudden desire to sleep with her made him blind to the woman's despair. And his own.

Everyone in the bar started singing at the tops of their voices:

The sun, I want the sun . . .

A song by Au Petit Bonheur, a group who were big at the time. Rico bought another round. The sun, yes, dammit! The sun!

They drank until the Chatham closed, at two in the morning. Julie wouldn't let Rico drive her home. He walked her to the taxi stand on Place de la République. Julie had slipped her arm into his and laid her head on his shoulder. They were both a little unsteady on their feet, both silent and unsmiling.

Driving back to Saint-Malo, Rico told himself they'd drunk so much, they wouldn't have enjoyed it anyway. The next time, he'd be careful. He really wanted her. He really wanted to love again. To rebuild his life. Why not? On the road—a straight, monotonous four-lane highway—he imagined days and weeks with Julie. Why not? he kept asking himself. Why not? He could still feel Julie's lips on his. A fleeting kiss that smelled of Oban.

Julie. They met again, two or three times a week, and the sequence of events was always the same. The place too. The Chatham, where they would drink until closing time. Almost without talking. Sometimes, they would move on to other bars, between Place des Lices and Place Sainte-Anne. Julie would respond to Rico's increasingly direct advances with "Not tonight" or "Some other time," all the while snuggling up against him.

After a month, Rico still knew nothing about her, or about her life. But he didn't give a damn. The way he told it to me, he was under her spell. Bewitched, and at the same time trapped, by his desire for her. A destructive spiral which in the end, although he wouldn't admit it, suited him.

One evening when they hadn't arranged to meet, Julie called him. From the Chatham. Rico could hear music playing. She was shouting into the receiver. She wanted to see him. To be with him. He had to get up early the following morning. He was going to Brest. It was fall, the time of year when he had the new collections to present. It wasn't a good idea tonight, he told her, they could meet in two days.

"Please."

A moan, which she was forced to scream into the phone.

"Julie . . ."

But she had hung up, abruptly. Shit! Rico had said to himself.

An hour later, the doorbell rang. It was Julie.

"Can you pay for the taxi?" she said as she came in. "It's six hundred fifty francs. He'll take a check."

She laughed. She was slightly drunk, and fantastically beautiful.

By the time he closed the door behind him, Julie lay sprawled on the couch. It was startling to Rico to see her there. In this house filled with dreams of another woman.

"Do you have a drink for me?" she asked, still laughing.

He poured her a drink, and one for himself.

She drank, then said, "Come."

As she snuggled up against him, her blouse opened and he saw the gentle curves of her bare breasts. Rico slid his hand inside, and his finger brushed against one of the nipples. It was hard and erect. With his other hand, he stroked her hair. She grabbed his cock through his pants, and squeezed it hard.

"Take it out," she breathed.

He pulled her down onto the floor, and managed to undress her. Her skin was dark and silky. He felt her quiver when he ran his fingers over her flat stomach, taut between her pelvis bones.

"Isn't there a bed in this house?" she asked, amused, as he slid a cushion under her back.

She turned to face him, and he felt her breath against his neck. Gasping and intense. When she drew him into her, Rico felt as if his cock was on fire. He came very quickly. Too quickly.

"Oh, no!" she cried. "You bastard! You bastard!" Then she pulled him down onto her chest. "It's all right. It doesn't matter," she murmured.

He closed his eyes and thought of all the times he'd had Sophie like that. It brought tears to his eyes.

"It doesn't matter," Julie repeated.

She was smiling. She made him roll over on his side. She looked straight at him with her dark eyes. They were empty of all desire, of all passion, as if covered with a dull film.

"If we get a move on, we can finish the evening at the Chatham, can't we?"

It was as he was driving back, alone, that Rico lost control of his car. Too many confused thoughts in his head and too much alcohol in his blood. He hit the barrier in the middle of the highway, bounced off it, and careered back across the road diagonally. A car coming from behind slammed into his rear, sending his own car into a spin.

On the radio, Alain Souchon was singing:

. . . I know it's all gone
But I still can't forget
And I sing till I'm breathless
Of all that regret

Then the radio stopped, and there was silence. And in the silence, his life came to an end without his even having had to turn the page. With that song echoing in his head:

All that regret, all that regret . . .

He and the other driver were both unharmed.

"You were lucky," the cops said to him, after the Breathalyzer test.

His licence was withdrawn for a year. He had lost his work tool.

He didn't see Julie again. He went to the Chatham several evenings running, looking for her. The barman there told him she often vanished like that. Sometimes for months. He didn't know anything about her. Except that it was always the same man who showed up to settle her debts.

12.

SOMETIMES, EVEN LOVE DOESN'T SOLVE ANYTHING

J ulie's real first name was Violaine. Rico didn't find that out until a few months later. But he could never get used to calling her Violaine. Even in his head. She was and would always be Julie. It was in Brest that he met her again, by chance. He'd been there for two days, visiting customers. As usual, he was staying at a small, unpretentious hotel called the Astoria, on Rue Traverse, not far from Cours Dajot where he liked to go for a pleasant stroll at the end of the day.

He saw her when he entered the hotel dining room. Julie. She was having breakfast, alone. She looked as if she was miles away, mechanically dipping a croissant in her cup of coffee. Rico watched her for a moment, then walked to her table. She raised her eyes, and the look in them was the same as when they had first met. Eyes to capsize the world, as Rico put it. All the things that had been making him feel heavy-hearted since the night of the accident vanished immediately. Just because of the way she looked at him.

"May I sit down?" he asked.

Julie nodded. She hadn't looked surprised to see him. Nor had she looked either pleased or displeased. And she was clearly not about to apologize for her silence. The only thing he could say for certain was that she wasn't indifferent to his presence.

"What are you doing here?" he asked her, feigning coolness.

"I came with my husband," she said unhesitatingly, in a flat voice. "He's a naval officer. On the *Foch*. He's just gone to sea again."

She looked at him over her cup, waiting for a question. Rico didn't ask any. He was overcome with emotion. And desire for her. What she had revealed of her life in those few moments was unimportant. The one thing that stood out was that her husband had just left, that she was alone again. He wanted to say, "It's great to see you." But she went on, in the same flat voice, "They're sailing down to the Mediterranean. I have to join him in Toulouse at the end of the week."

She put down her cup, then looked at her watch.

"I mustn't be late. My train leaves in an hour."

"That's the train I'm taking." He smiled, and lit a cigarette. "I'm going back to Rennes too."

"By train?"

During the two-hour journey, which they spent in the buffet car drinking whisky, Rico told her about the accident. How they'd taken away his driving license and now he had to travel by train from town to town to see his customers, and take taxis when he was in town. It took him three times as long as before to move around, he told her. It was a tricky business timing his journeys so that he didn't miss his connections.

"Brest to Caen," he said with a laugh. "You can't imagine what a nightmare that is!"

Julie was listening to him with obvious indifference, staring out at the landscape speeding by. As if her mind was on another life. Other misfortunes.

"I went to the Chatham a few times, hoping you'd be there."

Still she said nothing, and Rico started to get a little irritated.

"One of the barmen told me he knew you well. That there were times when you came in a lot, then you vanished, and your husband—your husband, is that right?—would come in and settle your slate . . ." He wanted to take her in his arms and hold her close. Instead he said aggressively, "And that you weren't shy with the men who bought you drinks."

At last, she turned to face him. "What of it?"

Rico would have liked it if she'd defended herself, denied

it, tried to explain . . . Anything, as long as she talked about herself. Just about herself. So he asked her the question he was dying to ask. "Do you love him?"

"No," she replied, coldly, looking him straight in the eyes.

"So why do you stay with him?"

"Because that's my life. Do you mind?"

Rico didn't insist, and they sat staring down at their glasses in silence until they reached Rennes.

"What are you doing now?" Julie asked him when they got off the train.

There was a local train for Saint-Malo in five minutes.

"I don't really want to be alone," she said, her dark eyes fixed on him. She seemed exhausted.

"My train leaves from the other platform," Rico replied. "Come on."

He took her by the arm and drew her toward his train, which was already waiting at the platform. She made no attempt to resist. The alcohol they'd drunk during the journey had again created a bridge between their two solitudes.

In the living room, Julie looked at the couch with an amused smile, then at the floor on which they had made love a few months earlier.

"So," she said, "is there a bed in this house?"

Rico laughed. "Yes, in my bedroom."

"What are you waiting for? Show me the way."

Her body seemed more fragile this time, her skin even softer. She trembled when he entered her. As if it was the first time she'd had a man inside her.

Her eyes, when she opened them, were not sparkling with happiness. They were like an ocean of sadness. But Rico was sure Julie had reached orgasm. They had made love slowly, until he had felt her nails plowing his back. But—and Rico did not realize this until later—they had used each other for their own pleasure, rather than taking pleasure in each other. The bodies of two strangers, enjoying a fleeting happiness.

"My husband killed the man I loved."

They had been lying there, smoking in silence. Julie was staring at some unspecified point on the ceiling. She had said these words in that flat, monotonous voice she had whenever she talked about herself and her life.

"Killed him?" Rico said in surprise.

"My husband scared him so much, with his gun and his threats, that he vanished, just like that. Didn't even say good-bye to me. Didn't say a word . . ."

"Was this before we met?"

She nodded. "A long time before. I was ready to give up everything for him . . . I'd been staying at my parents' place in Lamballe for two days. My husband drove all the way there. To take me home, he told my father."

She turned to the bedside table and grabbed the bottle of whisky that Rico had brought into the bedroom.

Rico ran his eyes down Julie's body. From her narrow shoulders to her small round buttocks.

She filled the two glasses and handed one to Rico.

"He slapped me in front of them, and they didn't say anything . . . They like my husband a lot. Having an officer in the family . . . that means something. The prestige of the uniform and all that . . ."

"Why did you marry him?"

"My mother doesn't understand what I have in my head. That's what she told me that evening, in the kitchen. She also said I ought to think about having children, like my sisters . . . who also don't understand me, by the way."

She finished her glass.

"It isn't love that matters. It's the appearance of love. That's how life works. All that ever matters is the appearance. Love . . ."

Rico didn't repeat his question. Now that Julie was talking, now that she was opening up to him the way he'd wanted her to do when they first met, he didn't know what to say. Or what to do. Or especially what to think.

He'd started wondering if what she was telling him was true. Or at least, how much of it was true. The more she revealed, the less he seemed to understand her. So he'd stopped really listening to her.

There was a moment when he imagined Sophie in bed with Alain, telling him about the terrible life she'd had with her husband, the way Julie was doing right now. Probably exaggerating how bad it had been in order to arouse his pity and win him over. No man, Rico thought, could resist hearing about a woman's disastrous love life. It was a thought that made him feel thoroughly sick.

"After dinner, when we were back in the bedroom," Julie went on, "he threw himself on me and pushed me back onto the bed. He raped me. You know what I'm saying? He raped me. He was saying all these horrible things, and I was yelling and screaming. He could have been killing me . . . But my father and mother didn't do a thing. I was his wife and . . . it was his right, he . . . That's what my parents must have been thinking too. My mother . . ."

Rico desired her again. In fact that was the only thing he was thinking about right now. The sight of her small buttocks a few moments earlier.

"Come," Rico said, drawing her to him.

"I can't," she murmured.

There was no emotion in her voice. She seemed to be looking at him from another world. A world where all passion was dead. And the last hope Rico had of making love to her again vanished.

"I have to go home. Will you call me a taxi?"

The following evening, they met at the Chatham and drank to excess. When the bar closed, she wouldn't let him come to her house, so they went in search of a hotel. They ended up in a room at the Atlantic on Place des Lices.

When Rico woke up, Julie was gone. He knew he would never see her again. Late in the night, he had said, partly as a boast, but mainly because he wanted her, "You know, your husband wouldn't scare me. If you wanted . . ."

"But I don't love you," she had replied wearily. "I don't love you."

Rico's blood had frozen. Julie had destroyed the last vestiges of life and hope remaining to him after Sophie had left. She had carried them away with her in her fall. Julie, as he realized later, had taken him to the edge of the abyss into which she had long since plunged. He had let himself be led. And his own fall came when he was summoned to Paris to account for his disastrous results for the first quarter of the year. The man who appeared at that meeting was a lost man. They didn't give him a chance.

Maeva's crying made Rico jump. He had settled again on the couch, after another swig of neat *pastis*. Now he got up. By the time Monique came into the kitchen, Rico had made more coffee.

She lit a cigarette and found a bowl.

"Up so early?"

She seemed less tired than the day before. Less nervous. More relaxed. Love calms you down, Rico thought.

"It's because of the kid, isn't it? She hasn't slept well all night . . . And you can hear everything in this place. The walls are paper-thin."

She looked at Rico, obviously wondering if he had heard them—and not just Maeva's crying. Of course he'd heard them humping. In fact, that was what had woken him. Dédé's long moans. Monique's shorter ones. Their pleasure had been like an echo of his own distant pleasures.

Rico shrugged. "It doesn't matter. I never sleep well."

They looked at each other again.

"Dédé's going to stay awhile, did you know that?"

"Yes, he told me."

That's how it was, Monique's eyes seemed to say. It was all a matter of chance. It didn't take away the weariness deep in her eyes, the sadness of her smiles. It wouldn't change any of life's absurdity. Her life was just as meaningless with Dédé as it had been with Jo. Except that it was more bearable when you were with someone. Whether that someone was Jo or Dédé.

"I have Jo's clothes, they'd fit you better than they'd fit Dédé. You can take them if you want to."

He had taken two of everything. Two pairs of pants, two shirts, two T-shirts, two pairs of socks. And a big navy blue sweater, sailor-style, with buttons on the left shoulder. He left the briefs, he preferred boxers. He put his dirty clothes in the garbage. Monique watched him.

"Are you throwing them away?"

It was a habit he had gotten into, thanks to Titi. At first, he had gone to the laundromat. Washing, spin-drying, tumble-drying. Twenty francs for twelve pounds. Plus powder. It worked out expensive, doing that every week. Especially as he never had enough for twelve pounds, but you still had to pay twenty francs. On top of everything else, you always had to have a spare set of clothes ready to change into. One day, at the laundromat on Rue de Montreuil, a young dropout had come in, stripped down to his briefs, started a machine, and sat down to wait.

Some of the housewives there had been outraged by this striptease.

"What?" he'd shouted at them. "You never saw the Levi's commercial?"

Of course they'd seen it. But it wasn't as funny in real life as on TV.

"On the street," Titi had said, "staying clean is more difficult than finding something to eat. And if you're not clean, you really go downhill. Because no one's going to give you anything if you stink."

"How do you manage?"

Titi had "his" bar. Every morning, he'd go there and have a quick wash. Forearms, hands and face. Clean his teeth. Have a shave. Once a week, he would go to the public baths on Rue Bouret in the 19th arrondissment. Six francs for a shower. With towel, wash cloth, shampoo and soap. And no one hurried you, no one came knocking at the door. Before that, he'd go to a cheap clothing store on Place de la République and buy a clean T-shirt, boxers and socks. Or a pair of jeans for fifty francs. "It's nice to have new clothes on your body," he would say. "Especially when you're clean."

Rico had adopted the same system. The only clothes he got from the Salvation Army and the Catholic charities were coats, jackets, sweaters and shoes.

"It's easier," he answered Monique.

They hadn't talked much the day before. But Rico didn't know what to say to Monique. It had been a long time since he'd last had any contact with a woman. And hearing her orgasm last night made him all the more uncomfortable now. He had no pressing need to go, and yet he couldn't wait to leave her and Dédé.

Félix was waiting for Rico in the lobby of the building, sitting on a step. The lizard's head seemed to be asleep. He had his ball in a big plastic bag with the words *Go Sport* on it.

He stood up. "I'll walk with you to the bus stop," he said, and the lizard's head quivered at the corner of his eye.

"Where did you get to last night?"

"I had to go over to the farm. Norbert has the flu, and Anne needed me. I like doing things for Anne. She's cute, and she's good to me."

It had snowed again, all night long. But Rico thought the temperature was milder than the day before. That might have been because of the hot shower he'd had, and the clean clothes he was wearing.

"Careful you don't slip!" Félix said.

"You could have come up and had a coffee . . ."

Félix shrugged. "You know, Jo asked me to keep an eye on Monique and the kid while he was away."

He was talking like Monique now. The same intonations.

"If it wasn't for that, I'd go with you to Marseilles. I'd have liked that. Great soccer team there. They're really good."

"Dédé's here now."

"Yeah, but he won't stay long. Anyway, I'd rather not talk about it."

13.

DAYS WITH AND DAYS WITHOUT,
THE FUTURE STOPS HERE

Rico had been wandering for fifteen minutes around the lobby of the Part-Dieu station in Lyons. Things should have been simple, of course. No different than for any other traveller. He'd looked at the indicator board at Chalon station and seen that there was a train leaving at 11:55 that would get him to Lyons at 1:12 P.M. From there, a high speed train would be leaving at 1:36 for Marseilles, where it would arrive at 4:18.

Rico could already see himself in Marseilles.

But when he got on the train at Lyons—Car No. 5, a smoking car—he came face to face with a ticket inspector, who immediately sensed who he was dealing with. He must have been trained to spot down-and-outs. Like those dogs who are trained to sniff out drugs in baggage when you cross a border. Because, washed and shaved, and dressed in clean clothes under his nice black parka, Rico looked like any other traveler you might pass on the platform. Admittedly, his faded blue rucksack, dirty and covered in stains, rather gave the game away. But not everyone traveled with Louis Vuitton baggage.

"Where are you going?"

"Marseilles."

"Can I see your ticket?"

Rico shrugged, with feigned weariness.

"You have to buy a ticket."

"I don't have any money, monsieur," Rico said, in as pitiful a voice as he could muster.

Sometimes the best thing to do was act humble. It made people feel sorry for you. It was a method he'd tried during his journeys from Paris to Rennes. They'd ask him for his papers, be about to fine him. What did he have to lose?

The ticket inspector looked him up and down. They were the same age, more or less. Two men from the same generation. But one had a job, a salary, and a little bit of power, and the other had nothing anymore, just a few things in a dirty rucksack. A tough nut, Rico thought, keeping his head down. He could feel the anger rising in him, as always happened when he came up against one of these people. What would it cost this guy to let him on the train? What difference would it make to the railroad company? To the economy of the country? The future of Europe? Why should it even bother him, dammit?

This ticket controller had an answer to Rico's questions. He probably had an answer to every question.

"It's not our job to transport every beggar in the world. Now get off the train."

He didn't say it harshly. But he did say it firmly. With all the authority conferred on him by the cap he was wearing. People were getting on. In a hurry, worried they wouldn't find a seat, or might even miss the train . . . Families. Old people. Men on their own. Women on their own. Young people. People with fair hair, dark hair. Africans. Arabs. Japanese. Each time, the ticket inspector smiled and moved back to let them pass.

"Excuse me," a young woman said to him, breathlessly. "I haven't had time to punch my ticket."

"It doesn't matter, madame. Take a seat and I'll be along in a moment."

His tone was affable and reassuring. In the spirit of the railroad company's advertising. You won't regret choosing to go by train.

"Get off the train," the ticket inspector said again. "Can't you see you're in everyone's way?"

It was true. Thanks to his rucksack, he was blocking access

to the seats. Some people were giving him angry looks. Others pushed him to get past. Shoved by a particularly corpulent man, Rico almost lost his balance and had to grab hold of the ticket inspector's arm.

"Please, just as far as Valence," Rico said, cracking a smile.

"I said, get off the train," the ticket inspector replied, pulling the sleeve of his jacket free of Rico's hand.

Suddenly, Rico had had enough of being humble. Enough of begging. He looked the ticket inspector in the eyes. Clear eyes, in which there was no emotion. Only indifference. And the coldness of regulations. Laws. Order.

"Fucking dickhead!"

Rico hadn't raised his voice. There was no hatred in it, or anger. Just contempt. A lot of contempt. The ticket inspector reacted as if Rico had spat in his face—which, in a way, he had.

"Get off the train!"

It was an order now.

Rico obeyed. The ticket inspector joined him on the platform. He wasn't smiling.

"If I see you trying to get on again, I won't let the train leave. Have you got that? Now get out of here, asshole!"

They weren't two men from the same generation anymore, they were men from two different worlds, with nothing in common.

Rico glared back at him defiantly. He imagined him at the depot in Marseilles, having a well-deserved cold beer with his colleagues and telling them the story. "There are centers for these people . . . They just have to stay in them, right? Instead of tramping the roads, especially in this cold . . ." Who would be offended by his lack of humanity? Who would say anything against a work colleague? A fellow union member? Then they'd have a few more beers, just as cold and just as well deserved, and talk about the thirty-five-hour week, family allowances, increased bonuses . . . At dinner that night, his wife might make a comment. "All the same, those poor people . . ." she would say. Even so, she'd end up siding with her husband. Because it was obvious: just like on the street, you couldn't give to everyone, you couldn't help the whole world.

"Stupid bastard," Rico muttered.

Then he turned his back on the ticket inspector, and set off back to the main lobby.

There was another train at 2:03 P.M., Rico noted. To Valence. From there, he could catch a high speed train at 3.44, which would take him to Marseilles. He set off in search of a bench. But they were all occupied. Or half occupied, like the one where a young couple was sitting comfortably, having a pleasant snack. He decided against disturbing them. The incident with the ticket inspector was enough for today. He couldn't take on the whole world. He didn't have the strength.

His sleepless night was starting to catch up with him. The pain in his back was flaring up again. It was a bad sign. He put down his rucksack against the window of a snack bar, sat down on the ground and opened a can of beer. He took a couple of Dolipran with the first mouthful. He'd taken the precaution of buying them that morning in Chalon.

Rico thought again about Dédé. In the middle of this lousy winter, he'd found a haven. A roof over his head, and a woman. It didn't matter how long it lasted, as Dédé had said, saying goodbye in the doorway. It was a victory over hardship. Then he thought about Félix, who had chosen to flee towns and people. To live in a cabin, in the middle of the countryside. With Sophie Marceau's smile to watch over him like a Madonna. Lizard's head, lizard's tail, Rico had murmured to himself, watching Félix, as motionless as if standing to attention, as the bus pulled away.

He was leaving him behind. And Dédé and Monique. It was a farewell. He'd never be back. Marseilles would be the end of the journey. The end of his wandering. The end of that disgust with life that had overwhelmed him since Titi's death. His self-disgust. Rico's eyes were closing. He remembered Julien looking at him through the rear window of Sophie's car. He tried to detect a gleam of hope, however tiny, in that look, didn't find one, and told himself that he was thinking too much, that it didn't help, that in any case there was nothing and nobody anymore. Nothing. Not anymore.

Someone shook him violently. Rico opened his eyes. Cops. There were two of them, as usual. A West Indian guy and a young woman. Shit! he moaned. Since the Homeless Persons Squad had taken him in once, he'd always managed to avoid the cops. He wondered if they had a hostel in Lyons like the Nanterre Center in Paris, where they stuck everyone they'd rounded up during the day.

"No sleeping in the station," the West Indian said.

Rico got heavily to his feet, still groggy with sleep. He looked at the station clock. Five past four. He had slept for two hours and missed the train to Marseilles. Others too, probably.

"Clear up that mess!" the cop ordered him, pointing to the can of beer.

Rico grabbed the empty can, slipped it into the pocket of his parka, and picked up his rucksack.

"Do you have your papers?" the lady cop asked.

Rico handed her his identity card folded in two. She unfolded it gingerly, glanced at the old photo, then stared at him.

"And do you have money?"

Rico showed her a hundred francs. An identity card and a hundred francs would normally have been enough. But from the way the two of them looked at him, he realized they weren't done with him. This really wasn't his day.

"Where are you going?" the lady cop asked.

"Marseilles."

"The ticket costs more than a hundred francs."

"I know."

"So?"

Rico shrugged. "I'll work out something with the ticket inspector."

"Oh, yeah?"

The two cops looked at each other.

"Follow us!"

Shit, Rico moaned again. He was angry with himself. He shouldn't have let himself fall asleep. He'd have seen them coming.

"My train . . ." he stammered.

"Just follow us!"

They escorted him to the police office at the station. There, they left him waiting on a bench.

"Taking us in is neither legal nor illegal," Titi had explained to Rico, when they had released him from Nanterre in the morning. "They take us in against our will, but of course they tell you it's for your own good. Legally, it's a mess, and it'll be a long time before it's cleared up . . ."

He remembered Nanterre with horror. Everyone naked. Carrying a bar of soap and a towel. On their way to take a compulsory shower. Under the eagle eye of a supervisor whose job was to make sure nobody refused. Then another corridor, everyone still naked. Trooping to a window where you were issued a dirty brown, stained, threadbare pair of pajamas for the night. Nanterre . . .

Cops came in, others went out. In the room they used as an office, he could hear them joking and laughing. One of them made a joke about North Africans in Marseilles, and they all roared with laughter.

Time passed. At six o'clock, the West Indian and the lady cop came for Rico.

"You, follow us."

Rico was at the end of his tether. He stopped complaining, even in his head, and let himself be led. He was resigned. His mind still full of images of Nanterre. Everyone in single file. Forced to tramp around the yard, waiting for dinner. One behind the other, silently. Like a procession of ghosts.

They left the station, and made Rico get into a white Renault 21. They drove through Lyons. A city Rico didn't know well. He'd only ever been there three times in his life. And he had never felt comfortable there. In the distance, on his right, he glimpsed the hill of Fourvière. He was starting to get worried.

"Where are we going?" he asked timidly.

They didn't say a word to him until they had left the city center and come to Pierre-Bénite, on the banks of the Rhône. Then they asked him to get out of the car. They were on the highway access ramp. Through the window, the lady cop handed him his identity card and laughed.

"We've put you in the right direction. If you know what's good for you, you'll get out of here as quickly as possible. According to the weather report, there's going to be a lot of snow. Have a nice journey!"

The car drove off. Abandoning him at the point where the ramp curved. No one would stop to pick him up here, even if they wanted to.

Rico felt the cold descend on him. He took his hat from his pocket and pulled it down over his ears, then raised the hood of the parka over his head and tied the cord beneath his chin. Automatic gestures. Survival mechanisms. He walked a few yards down the road and started trying to thumb a ride.

Since the cops had picked him up, his head had been running on empty. Of the hundred or so down-and-outs who must have been hanging around Part-Dieu station, they'd picked on him. Why? No reason. They just did, period. There were days with and days without, Titi used to say. The days with were like the future. So were the days without.

Cars and trucks sped past. Flashing lights. Honking of horns. The assholes were always amused to see some poor bastard at the side of the road.

A red Renault 5 moved very cautiously onto the ramp and slowed down as it passed him. The right indicator light came on. A little farther on, the car stopped. Rico waited before making a move. He'd fallen for that trick too many times. You walked to the car, and it pulled away just as you got to it. But this car was slowly reversing. Rico picked up his rucksack and went to meet it.

The door opened. There was an old guy at the wheel. The interior smelled of dogs.

"Where are you going?" he asked, starting the car.

"Marseilles."

The man laughed. "I'm only going as far as Vienne. Marguerite would be worried if I didn't come back."

"Your wife?"

"My dog. A Labrador. My wife's name was Louise . . . She preferred to go before me. She wouldn't be able to face being alone, she always said. Now here I am . . . and I can't die . . ."

"There's no hurry," Rico replied.

"I guess so. But there's nothing left to see that I haven't already seen, and what I see in the evening on TV doesn't made me want to hang around . . ."

He was driving slowly, in the right-hand lane. His head low over the wheel.

"I might be able to get a train at Vienne."

"I can drop you there. But it would have been easier at Lyons. Vienne's only a small station."

Rico had no desire to tell him about his encounter with the cops. "We can't always do what we want."

"That's what my wife always said. But where does that get

you?" He turned to look at Rico. "I don't mean that in a nasty way. Louise and I were happy. But we might have lived a different life . . . if we had wanted more."

Rico thought the old man was right.

"Anyway," the man went on, "I still have my dog. We're growing old together . . . As long as she's around . . ."

He threw a glance at Rico, then concentrated on the road. "You O.K.? You're not afraid?"

"I'm O.K."

There was a train. In half an hour. At 9:06 P.M. He would have to change at Valence. Thirty-eight minutes' wait, and then he could get a high speed train in the direction of Montpellier. Rico had no other choice. Either he spent the night in Vienne. Or in Avignon. It was easier to travel at night. The ticket inspectors were less of a hassle then. Sometimes, you didn't even see them. And Avignon was only an hour from Marseilles. He chose the second of the two options. He wanted to get as close as possible to Marseilles.

14.

AFTER THE SNOW, THE MISTRAL,
AND THE COLD, ALWAYS

It wasn't snowing in Avignon, but the mistral was blowing. Rico had no sooner set foot on the platform than he felt the cold go through him. He hurried to get to the underground passage to take shelter. There, in the corridor, he got his breath back.

There weren't many people in the lobby. Everyone was in a hurry to get home. Rico hesitated. Should he stay here and sleep in the station or head out into the mistral to find somewhere to crash until the first train for Marseilles? He became aware of eyes watching him. A group of young vagrants, with their dogs. Six of them, including two girls. All of them with shaven heads. Lounging near the phone booths, in the passage that led from the lobby to the station cafeteria.

Rico did not react quickly enough. One of the girls, a cigarette dangling from her lips, extricated herself from the group and came toward him, followed by one of the dogs, a mongrel with a face like a wolf. The girl stopped in front of Rico. She was wearing small gold rings in her ears and eyebrows and between her nostrils. She stank of grime and beer.

"Got a cigarette for me?" she asked, blowing her smoke into Rico's face.

The dog sniffed at Rico's shoes and the bottom of his pants. He's going to piss on me, he told himself. He had seen that happen once, at the Gare Saint-Lazare. There were vagrants who trained them to do it. They found it more amusing to see their dogs piss on someone's leg than against a tree.

He took out a pack of Fortunas, which he had bought in Lyons. They weren't expensive, but you couldn't find them everywhere. He held it out to her, but avoided looking at her. Her eyes were a dull blue, like dishwater. As dirty as her body must be. The girl took a cigarette, and stuck it behind her right ear.

"Can I take one for my friend?"

Now the dog was sniffing his crotch. Ready to bite him in the balls. Thing could easily turn nasty, he knew. Four guys, two dogs. If they decided to jump him, he wouldn't have anything left. And no one would come to his rescue.

"Yeah, O.K.," he said finally.

With the same action, the girl stuck the cigarette behind her left ear. There was a smile on her narrow, almost black lips. A smile as inviting as a razor blade. She looked just as degenerate as the dog, which was still glued to his private parts.

"You wouldn't have a hundred francs?"

"Have you taken a good look at me?"

One of the vagrants —the girl's boyfriend?—left the group and walked unsteadily toward them, a bottle of Valstar in his hand. He must have been about six and a half feet tall and weighed about three hundred and thirty pounds. A giant.

"Want a drink, friend?" he said, holding the bottle out to Rico.

Should he take it? Was the man trying to provoke him into a fight? The hand holding the bottle was broad and thick, the knuckles green with crusted dirt. Rico took the bottle and drank. He felt the girl's dirty eyes on him, the dog's muzzle sniffing at his crotch, from behind this time.

The giant laughed. "Welcome to Avignon, friend!"

The taste of the beer, and the fear gnawing at his stomach, aroused a craving for alcohol. He wanted to take another swig, but thought better of it. He had to get out of this station as quickly as he could. He gave the bottle back to the giant.

"That feels better," he muttered, adjusting his hat on his head.

"What's your name?" the giant asked.

"Rico."

The giant took the cigarette from the girl's left ear and stuck it between his lips. "Got a light, Rico?"

Rico took out his lighter and handed it to him.

"Know where you're going?" the girl asked.

"Drop it, Vera!" the man ordered, giving Rico back his lighter.

"Fuck you!" she cried. "I can do what I like! If I want to go with this guy and fuck him, I'll do it."

Things could blow up at any moment.

"You really piss me off!" the girl cried.

"I'm going," Rico said, as calmly as he could.

And, without looking at them, he walked to the exit. The dog went with him, its face against his calf. It let go of him when he opened the door and it sniffed the icy air. The man and the girl hadn't moved. They were still arguing.

Rico lowered his head and walked down the station steps, ready to brave the mistral.

Rico didn't know Avignon, so he had no idea which direction to go. He walked straight ahead. As far as the ramparts opposite. Porte de la République. He saw a sign: *Town Center*. The ideal thing, he thought, would be to find the entrance to an underground parking garage. Once past the ramparts, he walked along a gloomy, deserted avenue lined with plane trees.

The wind was so strong, it kept blowing him off his feet. Even with his mouth buried in the collar of the parka, he was getting out of breath. His eyes were tearing up. Every step required a considerable effort. He wouldn't get far like this, he told himself.

He saw a hotel sign: the Bristol. He set himself that as a target to aim for. He needed to stop and take a breather.

There were several bars still open on the avenue. Rico entered the first one he came to. The Régence. The light inside was yellow and harsh. He put his rucksack on the floor and sat down. He was gasping for breath. A waiter came up to him almost immediately.

"A draft beer," Rico ordered.

Apart from him, there were only seven customers in the place. All men on their own. He lit a cigarette and stared out at the street. He hoped this bar closed late. As late as possible. With the help of the beer, he could hold out all night. By the clock, it was midnight thirty. He had five hours to kill, or something like that, until the first train.

"Eighteen francs," the waiter said, placing the glass on the table.

"Eighteen francs for a draft beer?"

"Night rates."

"What time do you close?" Rico asked.

The waiter shrugged. "When the boss says so. If it was up to me, we'd already be closed." He gave Rico his change. "I'd rather be in bed."

"Sure," Rico said.

He took four Dolipran with his first swig of beer, and again stared out through the window. That was when he saw the girl crossing the street. Her head sunk between her shoulders, her hands in her pockets. Tight-fitting leather miniskirt, red pantyhose, and a matching blouse under an open suede jacket. Her long hair flying in every direction, covering her face.

Outside the bar, she straightened up, tossed back her hair in an angry movement of the head, then walked past the window of the terrace, looking in turn at each of the customers inside. Reaching Rico, she stared in at him with a kind of anger in her eyes. Without knowing why, Rico smiled at her. The girl went calmly on her way. As if the mistral didn't bother her.

Rico lit another cigarette and started thinking about the girl. About the anger he had seen in her eyes. He knew she was a hooker. But one who wasn't resigned to being a hooker. Or was still too young to resign herself to the idea that her life would consist of nothing but getting fucked by lots of guys. She couldn't have been more than twenty-five.

Rico was now the only customer sitting at a table. He had just ordered a second draft beer when he saw the girl walk past him again on the sidewalk. She came into the bar, and went and sat down at a table, not far from his.

"Lousy weather, huh?" the waiter said to her.

"Fucking weather, you mean!"

Her voice sounded weary, and she had an accent Rico couldn't place.

"Want a coffee?"

"A cognac. I've had my fill of coffee."

"We're closing soon, you know."

"Yes, I thought so."

She lit a cigarette and crossed her legs. Rico looked at her. From where he sat, she was in profile. She had a long face, but nice features. High cheekbones. Quite full lips. And a mass of shoulder-length ash blond hair.

She slowly turned to Rico and looked him in the eyes. Her own eyes were very dark blue, almost black.

"Like it?"

"What?"

"What you see. Me."

Rico smiled. "Yes . . . I do . . ."

The girl stood up, came to his table and sat down.

"Want to come to the hotel?" she asked, tossing back her hair.

The waiter placed the cognac in front of her. "Fifty francs," he said.

The girl did not move. The waiter looked from her to Rico.

"That's fifty francs," he said again, to Rico this time.

Rico counted out fifty francs from the coins he had in his pocket. His remaining money was in his left shoe, and he had no intention of taking it out like that in front of them.

"You been robbing a church or what?" the waiter asked, amused, as he watched him.

"No," he replied. "Just begging."

The waiter gathered the coins and walked away.

The girl raised her glass. "Cheers." She drank down half her cognac with her eyes closed, without drawing a breath. "You'll feel better afterwards."

"After what?"

"After we go to the hotel. If you want to come. It's not far. Rue Aubanel . . . It's just around the corner. Two hundred francs. Including the room."

"I don't think so . . ."

Rico saw anger in her eyes.

"Something wrong with me?"

"No, no . . . Not at all . . . But . . ."

She leaned toward him, and he felt her hair brush his cheek. It smelled of incense.

"A hundred for a blowjob. I know somewhere quiet we can go."

"I don't have money to throw away," Rico said, quite curtly.

The girl stiffened. It wasn't a nice thing for him to say. But he wanted her to give it a rest. He wished they could just talk. She knocked back the rest of her cognac and stood up.

"I'm wasting my time with you! Fucking bum!"

On her way to the door, she turned to the waiter, who had been watching them for the last few moments. "Bye, Max!"

"Bye, gorgeous."

Rico watched the girl as she went out. A gust of wind rooted her to the spot as soon as she was out the door. She sank her head between her shoulders, as she had earlier, and strode purposefully across the street. In a few moments, she was out of sight.

"We're closing," the waiter said.

Rico stood up slowly. It was only one o'clock. He'd have liked to sit here quietly in the warmth and have another beer.

The lights in the bar went out as soon as he was outside. As he still had no idea where to go, he crossed the street, like the girl, and walked back along the deserted avenue.

He came to Rue Aubanel. A dark, narrow street. He turned onto it and looked for the hotel the girl had mentioned. Where she turned tricks for two hundred francs, including the room. Maybe he could get a room for a few hours. He'd made up his mind that sleeping in a decent bed would do him good. He felt exhausted. He was ready to blow a hundred francs just to sleep.

Furnished hotel. Rooms by the day, the week, the month. He was standing outside an old building with peeling walls. All the lights were off. Above a bell black with grime, a notice read: *Please ring.*

"You following me or what?"

The girl's voice. He turned, and there she was. Her back against the wall, on the opposite sidewalk. Her head sunk between her shoulders. Her two hands deep in the pockets of her jacket, which she had finally buttoned.

"I was thinking I could sleep here for a few hours . . ."

"Oh! I really thought you were following me."

And she set off again for the end of the street, less energetically, Rico noted, than when she had left the bistro.

"It's filthy in there," she said, without turning around.

Rico followed close on her heels. She turned her head.

"You see, you are following me."

"Where are you going?"

"Home."

"Let's walk together."

She stopped dead. "What do you want?"

"Nothing. I have a few hours to kill, and I don't know where to go."

She started walking again. He followed her. They turned

right onto another street, and eventually came out onto a square. A bearded guy in a ragged coat stood outside a pizzeria, taking red, sticky spaghetti out of a garbage can and putting it in an aluminum container. He looked up as they passed, then put his head back inside the garbage can.

Now the mistral was behind them, and the girl was walking faster. Rico couldn't keep up with her. He was out of breath from walking so fast. She turned.

"Are you coming?"

The wind was tiring him out. Every gust seemed to penetrate his skull, freezing it from the inside.

"You're going too fast. I can't follow you."

"We're not there yet. It's a good fifteen minutes to my place."

15.

A PASSIONATE CLOSENESS,
LIKE BROTHER AND SISTER

Her place was a former hosier's shop. On Rue des Fourbisseurs. Rico had seen the street sign and had noted the name in passing, mechanically. As if it would help him to get his bearings in this town. Following the girl, he'd had the feeling they were going around in circles. Right now, he would have been quite incapable of finding his way by himself back to the main road—Rue de la République— along which he'd come when he arrived.

"It's here," she said, coming to a halt outside the old shop.

Rico was panting from having walked too much, too quickly, in the cold wind. He didn't immediately understand what she meant.

"It's here," she repeated. "I live in here."

There were big wooden shutters over the windows. Judging by their state, they hadn't been opened in ages. The varnish was peeling, almost obliterating the words painted on them, although you could still just about make them out: *Au Bon Chic Provençal—Established 1867.*

The girl entered the building through a little door to the right of the shop, and reappeared almost immediately.

"Are you coming or what?"

Rico joined her. He was a little disoriented. All he wanted was to put down his rucksack and go to sleep. Before the pain that was starting up again in his back got any worse and stopped him getting any rest.

"Push the door. The lock's broken, but I don't like to leave it open. You never know. There's no one in the building except an old couple on the first floor."

They entered the shop through what must have been the storage area. A corridor filled with shelves, now empty, which rose all the way up to the ceiling. The girl took a candle from one of the shelves and lit it.

"Wait, I'm going to switch the light on," she said, walking off with the candle.

Light appeared in the shop. A dim light, coming from a naked bulb that hung at the end of a wire above an old wooden counter.

"Romantic, isn't it?" she said ironically.

Against the wall, on the floor, a small mattress covered with a couple of army blankets. A canvas suitcase beside the bed. On it, a thick book, with a white cover, now yellowed. In the middle of the room, an old electric heater. And that was all.

"I've seen worse," Rico replied.

"Yes . . . Me too." She shrugged, then bent and switched on the heater. "Make yourself at home. I'll be back."

She disappeared into the corridor.

Rico relieved himself of his rucksack, then took off his parka and placed it carefully on the wooden counter. The heater emitted a series of cracking sounds as it grew hotter and the element turned red. He started to feel the heat, which was soothing after that walk in the cold wind. From the pockets of the rucksack, he took out the six cans he still had left. He opened one and took four Dolipran with a long swig of beer.

He looked around the room again. It was as sinister and depressing as his crash pad in Paris. But there was electricity, and a heater . . . What a strange girl, Rico thought. He had always supposed prostitutes had homes to go to, even when they had pimps who took almost all their money. Not her, and that intrigued him. But he was too exhausted to think about it. What did it matter anyway?

He again noticed the book on the suitcase, and couldn't help picking it up. Books reminded him of Titi, who often used to go around with a book in his pocket, which he'd either found in a garbage can or bought from a second hand bookseller. The last one was *The Théotime Farm* by Henri Bosco. He remembered it well, because Titi hadn't had time to tell him the story.

This one had a particular smell, a smell of damp and dust. *Saint John Perse: Collected Poems*, it said on the cover. He leafed through it until he came across a page on which a few lines had been circled.

A new race among the men of my race, a new race among the daughters of my race, and my cry as a living man on the road of men, step by step, from man to man,
To the distant shores where death deserts!

He closed the book, pensively. The words were beautiful, although he had no idea what they meant. He carefully put the book back on the suitcase, feeling suddenly embarrassed. He sat down on the floor, with his back against the wooden counter. He untied his shoes and stretched his legs toward the heater to warm the soles of his feet. He lit a cigarette and sat there, thinking of nothing.

The sound of a toilet flushing roused him from his torpor. The girl came back into the room. She had removed her make-up and put on a black tracksuit.

"The toilet's through there. There's a wash basin too."

"You want a beer?"

"I'll have a sip."

He handed her the can. She took a small gulp, then another, and gave it back to him.

"I'm bushed," she sighed, dropping onto the mattress.

She opened the case, took out a metal box and a pack of tobacco, and started rolling a joint.

"What's your name?" she asked, looking up.

"Rico. What's yours?"

"Mirjana."

"Where are you from?"

"Bosnia."

Rico tried to remember what he could of that war. Sarajevo under siege. A few terrible images. Words like massacres of civilians, internal migration, ethnic cleansing . . . Not very much. 1993 was the year Malika had dumped him. The year everything had fallen apart and he'd ended up on the street.

He looked at Mirjana. She had her head down and her hair in front of her eyes, and was carefully mixing the grass with the tobacco. Rico tried to imagine the road she must have traveled to get here. From horror to poverty.

From the worst to the least worst. But still the worst.

Hell. The street.

Mirjana twisted the end of the joint, lit it, and took a deep drag. She clearly enjoyed it. She held her breath for a few seconds, with her eyes closed, then released the smoke. Their eyes met. Hers seemed out of it.

"Want some?" she asked.

He shook his head. He had never smoked grass. Or ever taken any kind of drug. Apart from chewing a little *kat* when he was in Djibouti. To show off to his friends before a trip to the prostitutes' quarter behind Place Rimbaud. But he'd never overcome his fear and smoked a joint for pleasure.

"I'll stick with beer," he said with a laugh.

"I only smoke," she said. "I don't do anything else. Don't go thinking that."

She slowly blew out the smoke. The blue wreaths uncoiled above her head, and she watched them, then looked at Rico.

"I need it, after I . . . It relaxes me."

"Been working hard?"

He'd blurted it out. He felt embarrassed to ask a question

like that. But it was a way of approaching her. The simplest, most direct way.

As soon as their eyes had met, when she was on the street and he was sitting inside the bistro, he had felt close to her. A passionate closeness. Like brother and sister.

Rico was never able to explain to me what he had felt at that moment. Whenever he talked about Mirjana, he'd say, "A passionate closeness. Like brother and sister. Can you understand that?" I think he meant something beyond the fraternity of blood that you get in a family. He was thinking of another kind of fraternity. The kind that unites, somewhere between rage and despair, those who have been rejected. Excluded. That, anyway, was the kind of closeness I experienced with him. Like father and son.

Mirjana laughed. "Are you kidding? Two tricks the whole day. And a blowjob to a guy in a parking lot." She looked at the lighted end of her joint. "I prefer it when I'm fucking all day. At least then, I don't have to think, and I make some money."

Rico looked at her tenderly. The rings under her eyes were so dark, they were almost purple, and her eyes themselves, lost deep in their sockets, were without sheen. She seemed older than when he had looked at her in the bar. More fragile. Only her lips, when she talked, made her face look at all youthful. But it was as if it happened involuntarily. Her lips, her occasional smile, belonged to a world her eyes seemed to have left for good.

"You're falling asleep," she said, with a smile.

Rico's eyes were closing. The combined effect of his tiredness, the heat and the Dolipran.

"Yeah . . . I ought to sleep a little."

"Let's work something out."

She stubbed out what remained of her joint and pulled back the blankets.

"I have my sleeping bag," Rico said, getting it out of his rucksack, and unrolling it on the floor.

"You're not going to sleep like that! Put it here."

She slipped under the blankets and pressed up against the wall.

"Switch off the light, please. The heater too."

Rico slid into his sleeping bag and lay down. He hoped sleep would come quickly. Even with the blankets and the sleeping bag between them, Rico felt ill at ease. It was many years since he had last slept next to a woman. He didn't feel any desire for Mirjana, but she didn't leave him completely cold either.

"Are you O.K.?" she asked.

"I'm fine."

Their voices echoed, as if coming from somewhere else. From another world. From the shadows. From the cold. A world where things just had to be fine. Lizard's head, Rico thought before falling asleep. He remembered Félix. And Sophie Marceau's breasts, watching over him, watching over his dreams. He wondered what Mirjana's breasts were like, and the thought made him smile.

As was often the case now, since Titi had died, Rico didn't sleep for long. Just an hour. Time enough to drain away some of his tiredness. He was woken by a nightmare.

He was playing pinball. But he couldn't see his points on the scoreboard. Only countries, places he didn't know. Cities that didn't exist. And schedules that flashed by, like numbers on a lottery wheel. You had to hit the right targets to read a destination, a train number and its time of departure. Rico was feeling on edge. Marseilles just wasn't coming up on the board.

Behind him, he heard laughter. It was the ticket inspector. The pinball machine was on the high speed train.

The ticket inspector was laughing. "You'll never get there. Never . . ."

"Fuck you!"

Rico shook the pinball machine. Tilt.

The ticket inspector started giggling. "Never. Never . . ."

Rico grabbed him by the neck and started shaking him as hard as the pinball machine, then shoved him backwards. The ticket inspector fell down the steps of the train, which were suddenly as high as a skyscraper. He fell to the platform with the slowness and lightness of a dead leaf.

"Shit," Dédé said. "You broke his back."

Monique approached. She looked stunned. "Life," she moaned. "For murder, you get life. Life."

All three of them looked at the ticket inspector's body. His arms and legs were moving like those of a large beetle that had been rolled onto its back. People approached them. Some of them were people Rico had passed that morning at Part-Dieu station in Lyons. The vagrants from Avignon station were there too. Their dog started sniffing the ticket inspector's crotch.

"I'm going to find Félix," Dédé said. "He can borrow the van. We need to get the body out of here."

"Don't forget the pinball machine," Rico said. "We have to take the pinball machine with us. I need it. It's for the train, you see. It's time to catch the train. The train. The train . . ."

Rico sat up abruptly, as if propelled by a spring. He was sweating and out of breath. He groped for his cigarettes, which he had put down next to him. He turned on his side and lit one. He puffed at it gently, in order not to cough. Behind him, Mirjana moved.

"Can you give me a drag?" she asked.

"I thought you were asleep," he replied, handing her the cigarette.

"No. Too many things going around and around in my head. I'm afraid of having nightmares."

"I have them all the time. A friend of mine named Titi used

to say it proved that we wanted to carry on living. That we were still alive."

Mirjana gave a little laugh. "But I'm dead. I died a long time ago. When I saw them kill my parents. That's what I see. All the time. Them being killed. Just that moment." She turned. "But I'll kill him."

"Who?" Rico asked.

"The man who killed them. He was a friend of ours. He used to visit us. Him and his wife."

Rico didn't understand much of what Mirjana was saying. He wanted to ask another question, but she went on, in a low voice and a different tone, "I dreamed about you. I dreamed you were wandering in the dark, and so was I. We found each other."

"What are you talking about?" Rico asked in surprise.

"Nothing . . . It's from a book. A book I read a long time ago. It's weird, it just came back to me. Give me your hand."

Rico put out his cigarette, then held out his hand. Mirjana took it and placed it on her chest. On the side where the heart was. Despite the thickness of the tracksuit, Rico could feel her breast. He spread his fingers to feel the weight of it in his hand.

"Yes," she murmured. "I knew I'd meet you . . ."

Rico's fingers clung to Mirjana's breast. He could feel her heart beating. Every beat echoed in his body, his head. And in his own heart. Mirjana put her hand over Rico's.

"We may be able to sleep now."

16.

WE'VE FORGOTTEN HOW TO CRY WITH HAPPINESS

I find it less painful to feel like a stranger here than in my own country," Mirjana said.

Rico nodded, thinking about what Mirjana had just said. She was good at finding the right words when she spoke. Not that it made any difference to the mess human beings had made of the world.

According to Mirjana, there were about six thousand Bosnians scattered around the world. Most of them children of mixed marriages. They ended up in whichever country they could get to. Some were lucky, some found happiness, others didn't.

She had closed her eyes for a moment, and Rico had a sense of something somber behind her eyelids. The war, he thought. But the word was meaningless. It was only an abstract term, which didn't convey the tragedy of the situation, the reality of separation and death. The deaths of loved ones. The deaths of friends. The deaths of neighbors.

"There isn't a Bosnian suffering, a Serb suffering, a Croat suffering," she said. "It's the same suffering, Rico, can you understand that? . . . The same suffering . . . Common to everyone. The same pain . . ."

The sun was beating against the windows of the café. For a moment, its rays lingered on Mirjana's hair and surrounded it with a halo of light.

"But from what I've been able to gather, the predominant feeling in Bosnia now is one of hatred. Everyone feels obliged to hate the other communities in order to preserve their own . . . I don't want to live like that. I don't want to have to ask myself, when I'm walking down the street and meet someone, whether I should say hello to that person or spit in his face . . . I don't give a damn about being a Bosnian or a Serb. Or a Croat. What I want . . ."

She raised her eyes and looked straight at Rico.

"What I wanted was to be happy."

Mirjana had taken Rico to a little bar on Rue des Carmes. It was only just ten o'clock. When they had left the shop, the street was relatively deserted, probably because the mistral was still as cold and strong as ever. The sky was a pure blue.

"What a light!" Rico had exclaimed.

And he had stood there, like a boy, in the middle of the road, dazzled by the light tumbling from the sky, which forced him to blink.

The light of the South.

A strong icy gust had blown him a few yards off course. He had started laughing, and with his arms open had greeted the next gust by twirling around.

"Are you coming?" Mirjana had cried.

She had caught him by the arm and dragged him to the end of the street.

"You're crazy!"

"You have no idea! It's been months since I saw a sky as blue as this. And the sun . . ."

As they walked, Mirjana had taken Rico's hand in hers. He had given her a sidelong glance, but she had carried on walking as if nothing had happened, her head down against the wind.

The first thing Mirjana had done when she got up that morning was to gather her hair under a large red beret and put on a calf-length gray coat over her tracksuit.

"Let's go out for a coffee."

Standing there, with her hands in her pockets, she looked

like a schoolgirl who has grown up too soon. Rico had felt a gentle warmth suffuse his body. All she needed was a pair of glasses, he had thought, with a smile.

"What is it?" she had asked.

"Nothing . . ."

How to tell her what he was feeling? How to express the emotion he felt, deep inside? Rico had forgotten about these things, which belonged to a world of feelings. The words "I love you" and all the other sappy, infantile phrases people invent had gradually become threadbare. They evoked only memories. Fragments. Over the years, the flesh had decayed off those words, leaving only the bones. What did loving mean without the kisses, the caresses, without the pleasure two bodies can give each other until both are exhausted, until both reach that secret innermost point at which the word is annihilated in a cry and tears flow? "We've forgotten how to cry with happiness," Julie had murmured, the last night they had spent together.

Rico had wanted to say that to Mirjana. Just that one thing. But standing there in front of her, with his hands deep in the pockets of his parka, he couldn't utter a word, couldn't even tell her, quite simply, that he thought she was beautiful.

"Nothing," he had said again.

Rico had woken late. Mirjana lay with her face turned toward him. The room was dimly lit. He lay there for a few moments, looking at her face. Even in sleep, it betrayed all the tension inside her. She was asleep but not at rest. He had wanted to put his hand on her forehead, to calm her. But he had done nothing. For fear of waking her. There was no hurry. For her, as for him, the days were probably quite long enough already.

He had settled with his back against the wall, not far from the open door of the toilet, through which a little light filtered.

He'd had a beer, smoked a few cigarettes, and leafed through Mirjana's book, stopping whenever he found a passage under-lined in pencil.

The night opens a woman to you: her body, her safe harbors, her shore; and her previous night where all memory lies . . .

Once again, Saint-John Perse's poetry had dazzled him. Even if he couldn't grasp his meaning, even if it was beyond him, its music had unsettled him. He had repeated the phrases one by one. He had whispered them to himself, as if he wanted to learn them by heart. And as he recited them, he had been sure that Mirjana had savored each phrase in her mouth. And that, on her lips, the poet's words had become hers. At some point in her life, they must have found their meaning. In her.

Then Rico had thought again about what Mirjana had told him the previous evening. She hadn't said much about herself, about her life. But there had been so much anger in her words. So much despair. When you get to a certain point, Rico had thought, you can't turn back. Because you've seen things no one has seen, lived through things no one has lived through. You're condemned.

Condemned. Maybe that was the only response. The response to everything. Not wanting to return to that society wasn't a sign of powerlessness. Only of being weary of life after so much misery. Titi's death. Dédé's tempers. Félix's silences. What was the point of coming back to the surface of things?

When Mirjana had opened her eyes, Rico was holding the book on his knees, looking at her pensively. He'd been like that for a while, watching her sleeping, drinking another beer and slowly smoking.

"Oh, you're here," she had said, as if relieved to see him.

"Yes," he had replied. "I'm here."

And now he was listening to her.

The reason she had that book of poetry was because she had been a student of French literature. She had written a paper on Saint-John Perse. That book was her most precious possession. A lifeline she had clung to since the day she had been forced to flee Sarajevo.

"Those poems are the only reason I still have the strength to live. I know some of them by heart."

Mirjana took her purse out of her coat pocket. From it, she extracted a dog-eared color photo. The right-hand side of it had been cut off. She handed it to Rico.

"That was the last time we were together as a family. The next day, the Serbs started shelling the city."

She leaned across the table and pointed at the people in the photo.

"These are my parents. Manja and Miron. That's my aunt Leopoldina. This is my brother, Mico. And this is Selim. We were engaged. He'd just asked me to recite a poem, that's why I'm standing. It was Mico's wife Haidi who took the picture . . ."

Rico stared at the photo, as if hypnotized by the happiness that emanated from it. The image reminded him of other images, other family meals. His fingers started shaking.

"That's all I have left of the old days. This photo, and the book."

That was yesterday, Rico thought. And today nothing exists. Nothing will ever exist again. Not for her, not for me. The world dissolves, but not the evil that rules it.

Mirjana leaned even closer toward Rico, until she was almost lying on the table. She raised her dark eyes to him and gave him a look full of pain. Her lips almost against his, she started reciting, almost in a whisper:

I know you, O monsters! Here we are again, face to face, resuming that long debate where we left off.

*And you can advance your arguments like muzzles low on the
water: I shall give you neither pause nor respite.*

*On too many visited shores my feet have been washed before
dawn, on too many deserted beds my soul has been delivered to
the cancer of silence.*

For a long time, they looked into each other's eyes. Then
Mirjana slowly moved back, without taking her eyes off Rico.

"My parents were killed three days later. January 6th 1993.
The Serbs came to our apartment that evening. We were living
in Skenderia, in the heart of old Sarajevo. They refused to
leave, so they . . . They were dragged outside, and . . . 'You
can't transplant old trees,' Miron liked to say. My father would
never have left Bosnia. And my mother would never have
abandoned him . . ."

"But why? Why?"

"Why?" Mirjana shrugged. "All those things . . . They don't
matter now. The Bosnian Muslims did the same kind of thing
themselves later on . . ."

She lit a cigarette. Rico did the same. They smoked in
silence. Sometimes their eyes met.

Finally, Mirjana went on. "Selim enlisted on the first day. I
think he may have done terrible things too. Like so many people in Bosnia. Everyone was prepared for the worst, after the
nationalist parties won the elections in 1990 . . . Such madness!
I'll never understand it. My father often said that things happen
for reasons we can't work out. It annoyed me when he spoke
like that. I thought it was out of cowardice, complacency. But
now I understand what he meant. You can't do anything
against things you don't understand."

"What about your brother?"

"He took refuge in a chalet we owned in a little village
called Pazaric, on Mount Igman. Mico was stubborn too. He
wouldn't leave. Wouldn't try to get away. That was where they

arrested him. They imprisoned him in a gymnasium. For eight months . . . Then they released him. Since then . . . Even Haidi hasn't heard from him."

"Is she still there?"

"No. In Croatia. Haidi's parents are Croats. I spoke to her on the phone at Christmas. She seemed O.K."

She gave a little smile.

"I called her from a booth. She talked so much, I couldn't get a word in edgewise. 'Come . . . Come . . .' she kept saying. I saw the units getting used up, and then suddenly, nothing . . . Silence. I just stood there, staring at the receiver and crying. We didn't even get a chance to say Happy Christmas . . . Haidi . . ."

Abruptly, Mirjana stopped speaking and looked around her. As if surprised to be there, in that bistro. The place had filled up, and now smelled pleasantly of anis.

"Do you want to eat something?" Mirjana asked. "A sandwich? A *croque-monsieur*?"

Rico wasn't hungry. What he really wanted was a *pastis*.

They sat there talking and drinking—she drank coffee, he drank *pastis*—until Mirjana decided it was time to go to work. "Turn a few tricks," as she put it.

"I have debts. You can't imagine how much it costs, escaping, crossing borders. The most expensive part was getting to Italy . . ."

For the first time, something in her voice didn't ring true.

"I need the money. There are these Albanians I owe it to . . ."

Rico didn't know anything about all that. The traffic in illegal immigrants. But what he did know was that that no one ever gave anything on credit to someone in trouble. He wanted to say that to Mirjana, but changed his mind. Another question had occurred to him.

"Who is it you want to kill?"

"Dragan. My father's friend. He led the Serbs who came to the apartment."

Mirjana took her face in her hands. Rico thought she was crying, but it was only weariness. The weariness of pain.

"The only time I don't think about all that . . . is when I'm being fucked . . . I look at the guy sweating, trying to come, and I tell myself his life must be even worse than mine."

"And when you give him a blowjob, what do you think then?"

He had blurted out the words without thinking, and immediately regretted them. But it had revolted him that Mirjana could think such things. He could never find any excuses for the people who were always bugging him—the cops, the ticket inspectors. He could never forgive them for the way they behaved. That sounded too much like Christian charity. And it was a long time since Rico had last given a shit about charity.

"I'm sorry," he said.

Mirjana's eyes had blazed with anger. Then they had turned from dark blue to gray-blue.

"You know, I'll never forget that moment. When the shots rang out . . . I was just coming home. I saw Manja and Miron against the wall. The neighbors advancing. I cried out, 'Dragan! No! No!' . . ."

She lit another cigarette, puffed at it nervously, then searched in the pocket of her coat, took out a pistol cartridge, and held it out to Rico.

"I picked one up . . . Just one."

Her voice was ice cold. She placed the cartridge on the table, between them.

"They can't humiliate me more than I already have been. All the rest of it . . . The guys who fuck me are fucking a corpse. Never forget that, Rico. I died too. You know, Dragan was my godfather."

"Is that why the photo's been cut? Did you cut it?"

"Yes." She pouted in disgust, then flicked the cartridge so

that it rolled across the table toward Rico. "But I can't get his face out of my head."

Back in the shop, Mirjana went to the toilet to put on the clothes she had been wearing the night before. They hadn't said a word to each other since leaving the café. When she came back into the room, with her make-up on and her hair brushed, Rico was rolling up his sleeping bag.

She looked like another woman. He couldn't help giving her the once-over. More closely than he had done the night before, in that sinister bar. But with different eyes. Loving eyes, if the word still had any meaning for him. And he didn't like this woman.

She put on her jacket.

"You like me like this, don't you?"

"No, not really . . ."

"Oh? Why not."

"You should keep your beret on. I think it suits you."

"Oh, do you?" she said, surprised.

"Yes, I do."

They were both embarrassed now.

"Will you stay another night?"

17.

ETERNITY ONLY LASTS ONE NIGHT

After Mirjana had left, Rico felt lost. He stood there, helpless, in the gloom of the shop. She had asked him to wait for her, and he hadn't had to wait for anyone—especially a woman—for years.

On the street, waiting wasn't a problem. On the contrary. The more time you wasted—begging, or finding something to eat, or trying to get hold of a document—the better it was. Rico and the others had more time than they knew what to do with, and all those hours to get through in a day were too much for one man.

But here . . . The wasted hours would be gone forever. They would never return. Rico knew that. He knew his days were numbered. His days here, with Mirjana.

"What are you thinking about?" she had asked him straight out.

They were still in the bistro. Mirjana had managed to persuade Rico to eat something. They had ordered a cheese omelette for him, and spaghetti Bolognese for her. And a pitcher of local red wine.

"About you. About meeting you."

"And?"

He had shrugged. "It was strange, what you said last night. That sentence . . ."

Mirjana had closed her eyes and repeated, in the same tender tone, "'*I dreamed you were wandering in the dark, and so was I. We found each other . . .*' It's from a novel by an American writer, but I can't remember who . . ."

"What I can't get over is that you should remember it when I was there, or because I was there."

Mirjana's eyes, suddenly huge, had turned the color of the sky. Rico wanted to dive into them, let himself be carried deep inside her, to whirl around in her body and in her heart. That would have been easier than to put his thoughts in order and find words to express them. Easier too than to be forced to speak.

The more time passed, he had realized, the more difficult it was becoming for him to express himself. To construct sentences and put them in a logical order . . . His vocabulary was shrinking. Sometimes he didn't even get to the end of what he was saying. He would search for a word, not find it, and lose the thread of his thoughts.

But it was worth making an effort for Mirjana. He was sure she had expected that of him, Rico told me one day. She had expected him not to abandon all these things that were in his head to the street, to the misery of the street. That was why Rico talked to me every day. Out of loyalty to Mirjana.

Rico had filled their glasses. Then he had begun, slowly. As simply as possible.

"You know, Mirjana, I don't believe in chance. These last few months, I've had the same dream a hundred times, that I met you . . . I mean, that I met a woman . . ."

"Did she look like me?"

"No . . . no . . . How can I put it? This woman . . ." He made a sweeping gesture with his hand. "She wasn't a fantasy. If you see what I mean. She wasn't . . ."

"For jerking off to."

He'd smiled. "That's right . . . This woman didn't have a face. Or a body. Just . . . a voice. A soft, warm voice. And yet I could see her. Can you understand that? It was as if I could see her. And she was smiling. I imagined her smiling . . . And . . ."

He had broken off abruptly. He had just realized what the dream meant. The woman was a ghost. The ghost of his nights. And this ghost would take him by the hand. To guide him. To lead him. To the other side. Into another night. The voice would say, "Why aren't you smiling? Why won't you give me a smile?" And other words he didn't understand.

That was when he would wake up, always, bathed in sweat, shaking all over. He would drink, then go back to sleep. He would hear the voice again, just as caressing as before. The woman would again reach out her hand to him. Knocked senseless by alcohol, his mind would become dark and heavy. As heavy as concrete. And just as cold. One night, full of cheap vodka, he had become aware of how damp the darkness was. It had that characteristic smell of freshly turned earth, crawling with worms.

Mirjana hadn't taken her eyes off him. Nervously, he had downed his drink in one gulp.

"That's all. That's . . . all I remember."

His unease had seemed at that point to grow less intense, more remote. He had looked up at Mirjana. There was an incredulous expression in her eyes.

"That's all I remember, Mirjana."

She had lightly brushed Rico's hand with her fingers, sending a quiver first through his arm, then through his whole body, shaking him to the core.

"You have beautiful hands. I noticed them as soon as I saw you."

This remark had thrown Rico. His hands were big, broad, with prominent veins. Callous and grazed too. A down-and-out's hands.

"What's the point in telling each other these stories? I told you, Rico, it's as if I was dead. I don't know where you died. Or when. But you're like me, I know. We carry our old skins around with us, but inside we're empty."

Images flashed through Rico's head. Sophie slamming the door. The accident on the highway. Julie's tears. The apartment after Malika had gone. His second night on the street. His body rolling in the gutter. Julien's expressionless eyes . . . Then, in slow motion, a final image. Titi on a stretcher. Titi being taken away. The end of everything. Titi!

"Yes," he had admitted, wearily. "That's true . . . But we're neither of us at the end of the road yet. We each have one last thing to do. Yours is to go back and kill that guy. Dragan . . ."

"I don't know, Rico. Sure, I think about it a lot. When the pain is too much for me, I want to kill him. I keep saying to myself, 'I'm going to kill him.' To put an end to the pain. To rid myself of the hate . . . But what difference would it make, really? People would still hate each other. Today the Bosnians hate the Serbs. Tomorrow the Serbs will hate the Albanians. There'll always be people like Dragan . . . And Selim . . . I'm never going back."

Mirjana's eyes had shrunk to two luminous dots. Two golden irises. "This is the end of my road, Rico. Here with you."

Again, she was wrapped in that light that had dazzled him in the morning.

"And you?"

"Me?"

He remembered Léa's face. And her body. In the light of the setting sun coming in through the window of her small apartment near the harbor. He remembered her thrusting her thighs forward, sitting astride him, her back arched, her breasts offered to him . . .

"I just want to bring a memory back to life. A memory that looks like you, Mirjana."

He was sitting on the toilet, slowly smoking a cigarette. Two of Mirjana's panties hung from a nail above the wash basin, drying. Two plain white cotton panties. That made him smile. They seemed quite small to him, those panties, almost a child's, and he wondered how Mirjana could get her ass into them. He smiled again, at the inappropriateness of the thought.

He threw his cigarette butt down the toilet, then took off his left shoe and counted his remaining money. Four hundred forty-two francs. The money was slipping through his fingers, and he couldn't figure out how. He counted again, then tried to recall how he had spent so much money since leaving Paris with Dédé. He couldn't do it. The figures didn't add up. Finally, he gave up. In any case, the conclusion was obvious. He'd have to think about begging again. The idea turned his stomach. Just as much as when he'd had to resign himself to it the first time.

He thought again about Titi. About his advice, which had helped him. But in the end, the advice didn't mean anything. He knew that. One Sunday, Rico had seen Titi begging. On Rue d'Aligre, outside the covered market. Limping towards people, his hand held out, pitifully.

"Hey, Jacques, you wouldn't have a little something for me?"

Rico had seen himself in Titi. It was as if he was looking at himself in a mirror. It had taken him a while to forget the image. An image of how he himself would be, one of these days. It had taken him a while too to summon up the courage to start begging.

When he'd finally resurfaced, Titi had asked him, "Where on earth have you been?"

"Oh, you know. Took a trip down to the Riviera."

"Oh, yeah. I see. Things not going well, eh?"

"I can't beg anymore. It disgusts me."

"I'll tell you something, Rico. When a man's at the end of his tether, he begs, but when a woman's at the end of her tether, she sells her body. Just think of that. Any humiliation you may feel is nothing compared with what they must feel. Getting fucked for a living, we can't even imagine what that must be like."

"Mirjana," he murmured.

He clenched his teeth. With anger. At himself. At mankind. Assholes, all of them . . .

"Assholes!" he cried. "You're all assholes!"

Furiously, he folded three hundred-franc bills and put them in his shoe, then went out to get beer and cigarettes. He didn't see how he could wait for Mirjana to come back without anything to drink.

Rico spent the rest of the afternoon like that: drinking, smoking, dozing on the mattress, in the gloom of the shop. Increasingly disgusted with other people as he was, he felt calmer. Even his memories had stopped hurting. It was as if things were finally falling into some kind of order in his head. And this order gave a meaning to everything.

Late in the afternoon, or early in the evening—he had no idea what time it was—he fell asleep thinking about Mirjana's little panties, while a line from Saint-John Perse hovered in his head:

I had, I had this taste for living among men, and now the earth exhales its foreign soul.

When Mirjana came back, she found him sitting on the mattress with a blanket over his shoulders, reading. The ashtray was full to bursting, and there were six empty beer cans next to it.

In one hand, she was holding a flat, square box. In the other, a bottle of red wine.

"Pizza!" she said, putting the box and the bottle on the floor. "And Côtes du Rhône!"

He stood up. "What time is it?"

"Ten o'clock."

She took off her beret, threw it down angrily on the mattress, and lit a cigarette. She was on edge.

"I've had it up to here. The idiots are all watching TV. I didn't even know there was a match. Marseilles-Lens, I think it is. Can you imagine, one guy wanted me to give him a blowjob in his car so he could still follow his fucking game!"

Rico looked at her. No, Titi, he said to himself, we'll never know anything like the humiliation women go through.

"The assholes!" she cried.

She went off to the toilet. When she came back, she was wearing her tracksuit. She had removed her make up, brushed her hair back and gathered it in a pony tail. She switched on the heater.

"Let's eat. I'm hungry."

They had finished the bottle.

"I should have bought two," Mirjana said apologetically. She was rolling a joint.

"I have some rum," Rico said.

He stood up to get his rucksack. He removed the sleeping bag and pulled out a half-pint bottle. A brand called La Martiniquaise. You'd do better to flambé bananas with it than drink it, but at least it was cheap.

"Do you keep everything in your rucksack? Don't you leave anything lying around so much?"

"It's what comes of moving around."

She took a swig of rum, grimaced, then concentrated on her joint. She twisted the end, lit it, and happily inhaled the smoke. She took a second, gentler drag, then put her hand on the back of Rico's neck, and drew him to her. To her mouth. He let her do it. He closed his eyes. Mirjana's full lips brushed against his. He opened his mouth at the same time she did. The smoke hit the back of his throat. He breathed it in, then immediately pulled back, making an effort not to cough.

He opened his eyes. Mirjana was smiling. She took another drag, for herself.

"You see," she said. "It's the same with everything. You mustn't be afraid."

*

Later, they both lay down under the blankets.

"Come," Mirjana had said.

She lay huddled against him, her hand on his chest. He breathed in the smell of her hair. A smell of shampoo and cold cigarettes.

Slowly, Mirjana unbuttoned Rico's shirt. In his head, all the memories started to mingle and become confused. When Mirjana's fingers brushed against his chest, he jumped, as if he had just had an electric shock.

"How long has it been?"

"A long time."

She opened Rico's shirt wide, put her cheek against his skin, and let her fingers glide over his stomach. Rico's memories seemed to have been chased away, pushed far back in his mind. Behind that horizon line, imaginary perhaps, where nothing else mattered but the present moment. Now his mind was like a clear blue sky. A mistral sky. He thought about love. About what love was. The pleasure of loving. The tenderness of days. The gentleness of moments. What shared happiness meant. That ever-necessary, indispensable lightness of words and gestures and thoughts.

"Do you want to make love?"

Rico turned to Mirjana. His eyes searched for hers in the darkness. "What do *you* want?"

She snuggled up to him and held him tight.

"We don't have to do anything," Rico said. "We're fine like this. It doesn't matter, all that . . . I like to feel your fingers on me. They're so soft."

"That's what I want too. Your hands."

They undressed each other, and when they were naked, they slowly caressed each other. They had the whole night before them. An eternity. An eternity just for them. One night.

At one point, Rico felt Mirjana's tears on his shoulder. Tears of happiness. He remembered a song, revived by Bashung, I think, and started singing in Mirjana's ear.

I'll tell her words that are blue
Words that make us all brand new
I'll tell her all the words that are blue
All the words that make us brand new
all the words that are blue
all the words that are blue . . .

18.

FOR THE LAST PERSON WHO DIES,
EVERYTHING WILL BE EASIER

The door burst open. As if smashed in by a bulldozer. Rico was sitting on the floor, reading, just like the previous day, near the door to the toilet. He leapt to his feet. Mirjana, who had been sleeping, sat up abruptly on the mattress. Distraught. In a panic.

"What is it?"

Before she had time to react, two men came charging into the shop. The heavier, more thickset of the two was in jeans and a brown jacket. The other man was taller and thinner, and wore a long black coat. He walked into the middle of the room with his hands in his pockets and a smile on his lips.

"Fatos!" Mirjana cried.

She wrapped herself in the blanket and looked around for her tracksuit. She saw Rico walking unsteadily toward the two men.

"What do you want?" he yelled.

"Rico, no," she stammered.

But the heavy guy had already thrown himself on Rico and grabbed him by the neck.

"You just keep your mouth shut, O.K.?"

And he shoved him out of the way.

Rico's back hit the wall. It took his breath away. He felt his legs give way, but he didn't fall. He stood there with his back against the wall, dazed, gasping for breath.

Fatos went up to Mirjana, put his hand on the back of her neck and grabbed her by the hair. The pain made her cry out and drop the blanket. He pulled her into the centre of the room and let go of her.

Mirjana stood there, helpless, making no attempt to hide her private parts with her hands. She held herself straight, with her head high.

"Hello," Fatos said.

Now Rico understood Mirjana's silences in the bistro the day before. The ambiguity of some of her explanations. He looked from Mirjana to Fatos.

"No panties even . . ." Fatos turned to the heavy guy, who was standing behind him, keeping an eye on Rico. "It was worth the journey, don't you think, Alex?"

"It sure was!"

From the way he said that, it was obvious he was already imagining sticking his dick into Mirjana.

"Fatos," Mirjana said again. The fear had gone from her voice.

"You didn't make it easy for me to find you, you know."

And he slapped her full in the face. The impact almost made Mirjana lose her balance. She took a few steps back and rose to her full height. Her head was still held high.

"But as you can see, I found you in the end."

He hit her again, just as hard, with the back of his hand this time. A few drops of blood appeared on Mirjana's cheek, caused by the big signet ring Fatos wore on his right hand.

"Leave her alone!" Rico screamed, finally getting his breath back. "Leave her alone!"

"Who is this clown?" Fatos asked.

"This has nothing to do with him," Mirjana said.

"I asked you who he is."

"A guy I met . . . In a bar." Her voice was harsh, toneless.

Fatos turned to face Rico. He looked him up and down, with a disgusted expression. The threadbare jeans, the old sailor's sweater Monique had given him. Their eyes met. Fatos's horrible dark eyes contained all the vileness, all the meanness in the world.

"A night with her isn't cheap. Did you know that, asshole? I hope you have the money to pay for her!"

"He didn't have anywhere to sleep," Mirjana said.

Fatso turned back to her. "You take your clothes off for bums now, do you?"

Fatos raised his hand to slap her again. Mirjana saw it coming and tried to dodge it. Fatos's hand hit her temple. Hard. Dazed by the blow, she swayed.

"Leave her alone!" Rico cried again.

He wasn't afraid of being hit. He didn't stand a chance against these two guys, but he didn't care. He was filled with rage. And hate. It was always the same shit, everywhere you went. He stood with his back and ass against the wall, ready to jump them. Ready to attack. But before he could do anything, Fatos, as if he knew what Rico was planning, clicked his fingers and pointed at him.

Alex walked up to Rico and punched him hard in the stomach. Once. Twice. His fists were like steel. Rico was again thrown against the wall. Flashes of white light exploded under his eyelids. This time, his legs abandoned him and he slid down the wall. Like a slug. Rico had that image of himself, as he collapsed on the floor.

Bent double, his eyes half closed, he tried to get his breath back. His stomach seemed to have set off an avalanche of hard stones. With sharp edges. With each breath he took, all these stones ripped his lungs apart then rose to his throat. Choking him. Mouth open, foaming, he gasped for air.

"Get dressed!" Fatos ordered Mirjana. "You look pitiful."

She went to pick up her tracksuit, which was lying rolled up at the foot of the mattress. She moved without hesitation. Then she caught Rico's eye, and her movements became slower. For a moment, she even seemed to remain motionless. Until she pulled the tracksuit up over her pubis. But that slow motion may only have existed in Rico's head. At that moment, he told himself he would have to get used to the idea that he would never see Mirjana again. Just as you do when someone has died.

Fatos walked up to Rico. With the tip of his shoe—an impeccably polished black shoe with a gold buckle on the side—he turned Rico's face toward him.

"The woman is mine. Have you got that, asshole? I bought her. In Taranto. And I paid a lot for her. Far too much to let her be fucked by losers like you."

Rico tried to look at Mirjana again. He saw her pulling on the tracksuit top.

"Look at me!" Fatos said.

The tip of his shoe slid from Rico's cheek down to his chin. Fatos exerted a little pressure.

"She wanted to see Paris," he said, laughing. "The Eiffel Tower. The Champs Elysées. The Galeries Lafayette . . . All that crap. But it all costs money. Do you know that, asshole?"

The tip of the shoe moved up to Rico's nose, with the heel wedged under his chin. Fatos pressed.

"Leave him alone," Mirjana said. "You found me. Isn't that enough for you?"

"I've lost a lot of money. More than three months' income, Mirjana. Plus all the money I spent trying to find you. Grenoble, Lyons, Marseilles, Arles. I looked everywhere for you. You can't imagine how much it cost! And you go and fuck a loser like this."

Fatos's shoe pressed more heavily against Rico's nose and chin.

"You found me," she said again.

Fatos took his foot from Rico's face and put it down on the floor.

"Yes . . . That's true, that's true . . ."

Fatos's leg shot out, and his foot hit Rico full in the face. On the nose. More flashes, red this time, streaked across his sight. The impact made him close his eyes. Blood gushed from his nose.

"I have money!" Mirjana cried. "I've been working!"

She was scared now. Not for herself. For Rico. She had realized that it wasn't her Fatos was going to beat, in order to get his revenge, it was Rico. She was one of his meal tickets. Rico was nothing.

"At last you're talking sense. How much have you made in all this time?"

Mirjana opened her suitcase. From it she took a small blue canvas bag, put her hand in and pulled out a handful of banknotes. Hundreds, tens, fifties . . .

"About ten thousand, I think. I haven't counted. This is all I've earned. I haven't spent any of it, Fatos. I haven't spent any of it."

"Ten thousand . . ." He turned to Alex. "Here, count it!"

"You see," Mirjana said.

"What do I see?"

"There's money. It's what you wanted."

Mirjana took a step forward.

"Where are you going?"

"He's bleeding," she replied, pointing to Rico. "I—"

"Don't move."

Fatos lit a cigarette, took a long drag, then held it out to Mirjana. She shook her head.

"It's up to you."

"Nine thousand two hundred," Alex announced.

"Nine thousand two hundred . . . That's not ten thousand . . . In my opinion, Mirjana, you've been selling yourself cheap. Unless you've spent your time fucking every bum you picked up from the gutter."

With great speed, Fatos swiveled and again kicked Rico. In the stomach this time. Rico let out a cry. Or rather, a moan. His eyes misted over. Fatos lifted his foot again.

"Stop!" Mirjana screamed hysterically. "Stop!"

Fatos's foot came down to within about four inches of Rico's stomach.

She threw herself to her knees in front of Fatos, her ass on her heels. She was crying, with her head down and her shoulders hunched. "Please."

Fatos stubbed out his cigarette on the floor, then crouched by Mirjana, took her chin in his hand and forced her to look at him.

"You're just a stupid bitch! That's what you are! I'm putting you to work at Barbès. You'll be fucked by Arabs and niggers all day long. Get the idea?"

Rico was listening, his eyes streaming with tears. He remembered the vagrants at the station. The girl, and her fucking mongrel dog sniffing his crotch. He'd have liked to have that dog with him right now. He'd have liked to see its jaws close over Fatos's balls.

A dog! Rico screamed to himself in his head.

He slowly relaxed his legs and slid his feet toward the wall. He braced himself against it. He gathered what little strength he had left, and all the hatred he felt.

I'm a dog!

He released the tension in his body and leaped. Jaws open. Fangs out. Foaming at the mouth.

A fucking dog!

He aimed for Fatos's throat and sunk his teeth in his neck. Fatos screamed. Alex started kicking Rico in the back and punching him on the head. With each blow, the flashes split his eyes. His head. White. Red. White. Red. Red.

Red.

And the blood.

Then, suddenly, Rico didn't feel anything anymore. He had let go.

"Fucking asshole!" Fatos cried.

Blood was gushing from his neck.

He kicked Rico again. On the chin.

"That's enough," Alex said. "That's enough. He's had what was coming to him."

He bent over him. He'd stopped breathing.

In Rico's head, he felt how damp the darkness was. The black ground, crawling with worms.

No. Not now, no.

Why aren't you smiling?

Not yet.

Why won't you give me a smile?

No.

The taste of blood on his lips. In his throat. Fatos's blood. And his own.

"No," he moaned.

"We have to get out of here, Fatos. I think he's dying."

"Rico."

That soft, caressing voice.

Mirjana was sobbing.

She hadn't stopped screaming. Begging.

She kneeled beside him. Her lips against Rico's ear, she whispered, "I'm dead, don't forget. Dead . . ."

She kissed him on the forehead.

Fatos grabbed her and pulled her off him.

"Take your things, and let's go."

Rico heard the zip of the suitcase being closed. And footsteps. Their footsteps.

He couldn't open his eyes.

To see her one last time.

Mirjana.

"Bastards," he muttered.

But no one heard him.

Everything went black in his head.

Darkness.

Rico said, one evening when we were looking at the sea, "When Titi died, it was as if something of myself had gone. With Mirjana . . . You know something, Abdou? It'll be easier for the last person who dies. Because he'll already have lost everything."

PART TWO

19.

SHALL WE GO DOWN TO THE SEA?

I'm Abdou.

I've been scuffling in Marseilles for two months now. I'm Algerian. From Algiers. I'm thirteen. Well, that's what I tell people. I may be fourteen, or fifteen. As I don't have any papers, I can't be sure. But I don't give a damn about my age. It doesn't make any difference to my life. That's what I told Rico, the day we met.

It was a cold, gray January afternoon. We were sitting on a bench on Place de Lenche, in the Panier, the old quarter near the harbor. Rico was out of breath from walking all the way.

"Yes," he said. "You're right. You're as old as you feel."

"As old as your peter," I said.

We both laughed.

I liked to make Rico laugh.

I'll never forget the way we met.

I was coming up Rue Caisserie. A street that takes you all the way around the hill of the Panier.

Rico was glued to a billboard. A poster for a brand of women's underwear called *Aubade*. The poster showed this fantastic woman's ass, two nice plump mounds, thrust right out under the noses of passers-by. It really stopped you in your tracks, I can tell you! Especially as the girl's tiny panties, a few little wisps of lace, were stuck right inside the crack of her buttocks, making the two mounds even more mouth-watering. At the bottom of the poster were the words: *Lesson No 27. Create an area of turbulence.*

I'd come to a standstill behind Rico. As hypnotized as he

was. Even now, when I close my eyes and imagine how it would be if a girl really did show her ass to me like that, I quickly go from a "state of agitation and disorder"—that's the definition of turbulence, I was in a bookstore once and I looked it up in a dictionary—to a complete earthquake! To this day, I don't know what the previous lessons were, but *Aubade's* No. 27 always makes me want to jerk off.

Rico must have sensed me behind him. He turned, looked at me in surprise, then pointed to the poster. "That's my wife's ass. Sophie."

"Interesting," I replied.

"Yeah . . . Especially if you can stick your cock in there. I forgot it was so . . ." With his hand, he drew the wonderful curve of the lower back and buttocks in the air. "Wow!" His hand fell again, as if exhausted. "It gave me a shock!"

"No kidding, that's really your wife's ass?"

"Yes, it is! Well . . . I mean it's . . . It's like Sophie Marceau's breasts . . ."

I couldn't see the connection.

"You don't understand . . . Look . . ." He practically pressed my nose to the poster. "You see the texture of the skin? It's the same. Identical. Her twin, that's what this is. Her twin." He took a few steps back. "Sexy ass, don't you think?"

"Sure is!" I laughed. "Hey, you were some lucky guy."

"Yeah . . ." he said, wearily. Without taking his eyes off the poster, he lit a cigarette, a Fortuna. "Yeah," he said again, turning to me. "Since then, her ass has fallen into other hands. Enemy hands."

I laughed. "The world is full of backstabbers."

Rico laughed too, then he started coughing fit to burst. "You're right, the backstabbers take everything and leave you with nothing. The poor are the worst. They'd even steal the crumbs from your pockets . . ." He shrugged. "Are you from around here? I think I've seen you before."

I liked it when he said that.

Since I'd started bumming around Marseilles, I'd often run into Rico in this neighborhood near the Vieux-Port, and had gotten used to his weird appearance. Wrapped up in his black parka, with his navy blue woollen hat pulled down tight over his head, he'd walk along with his back bent, looking into the distance, dragging a grocery cart behind him. One of those little carts with a canvas bag on them, the kind you see women use when they go shopping. I never saw Rico without his cart. Always full of newspapers, knick-knacks, old books that people gave him or that he picked up here and there on the street.

Until Rico died, the Vieux-Port was my favourite place for a walk. The perfect remedy for feeling stifled—the *ghoumma*, we call it in Algeria, like when your folks won't let you go out.

I'd walk as far as the Fort Saint-Jean, then along the sea wall, until I reached the entrance to the channel. Where the sea begins. With the horizon in the distance. And Algeria on the other side, the other shore. I'd settle comfortably in the rocks, light a joint, and spend hours daydreaming.

Marseilles—that part of town, anyway—always reminded me of Algiers. Not that I felt homesick. My home doesn't exist anymore. I'll never set foot there again. I want to forget Algiers. But I needed to hang on to a few memories. That's all I have left, a few memories.

I wasn't the only one reliving their memories here. Lots of guys hung around the Fort Saint-Jean, alone or in groups. Quite a few Algerians like me. But also Africans, Turks, Comorians, Yugoslavs . . . A guy who tried to sell me dope told me he thought Marseilles looked like Dubrovnik. "It looks like any place you want it to look like," I replied. How we all end up here is another story. But I've never beaten myself up about that.

Sitting quietly among the rocks, I'd close my eyes and see myself with my pal Zineb, at the Eden or the Deux-Chameaux, bathing all summer. And it really made me feel good to think about him. Especially like that, diving into the lukewarm water of the harbour. Shouting and laughing. Whistling at the girls . . . It was a comfort, you know? It calmed me down when I felt like setting fire to this whole fucking shitty planet. If I'd had good enough matches, I'd have done it long ago.

"You haven't answered my question," Rico said. "Do you live around here?"

Ya Khi blad yak hi! Fucking country! I woke up from my daydreams. Rico was looking at me. It was weird, the way he looked at me. As if he didn't notice the burns on the left side of my face, the eye almost down to the chin. It was the first time that had happened. With everyone else, even the kindest of them, I knew they couldn't take their eyes off those lousy marks when they talked to me. They all found them repulsive.

"I'm just passing though," I replied.

"You come and go, right? Like me."

"Right."

"And where were you going?"

"Down to the sea."

He smiled at me. "The sea? That's on my way."

He grabbed hold of his cart and started walking slowly. I followed him. I didn't really care where I went.

The head of a teddy bear protruded from the cart. One eye hung loose and rocked gently as the wheels turned. It was a nice effect. As if the bear was winking.

"Where did you get that bear?"

"Someone just gave it to me. It's a collector's item."

"I never had one."

Rico stopped. He looked at me again, right in the eyes this time. "I can't give it to you, you do realize that?"

"Hey, I didn't ask you for it!"

"That's all right, then."

He started walking again, and we carried on like that until we got to Place de Lenche. There he suggested we take a breather and sit down on a bench. He was too out of breath to continue.

"I always take a breather here. I like this square. It's nice here, don't you think?"

He wedged the cart between his legs, and closed his eyes. His breathing was halting and wheezy. It was really painful to hear him breathing like that. I sat there without moving, without saying anything. The bear stuck its tongue out at me, a little tongue of red cloth. "Hi, Zineb!" I said.

Rico had been in Marseilles for nearly a year. Physically, I think, he'd changed. He was as thin as a rake. The lower part of his face was covered with a salt and pepper beard, which he'd let grow so that he didn't have to shave anymore. Wisps of greasy hair peeped out from under his hat. And when he smiled, in that gentle way he had, you could see his teeth were black and decaying.

Obviously I didn't know it just then, but Rico looked like Titi. The way Titi had been at the end, the way he later described him to me. And the way I imagined him in my head. A bum. Rico just didn't care about anything anymore. Even his black parka, which he was so proud of, was threadbare and covered in stains. It had aged, just as he had. Just as quickly as he had. And he never took it off. Whatever the weather. I think he even slept in it.

Gradually, Rico's breathing became more regular, almost normal. He opened his eyes, took out his cigarettes, and offered me one.

"So where do you crash?"

"At the Ozéa. It's a hotel on Rue Barbaroux, not far from the Canebière. There are four of us per room, sometimes five."

"And how did you end up there?"

"Through a center called the Young Strays. It isn't a shelter. There are no dormitories, no canteen. They call it a walk-in center. A place you go to when you don't know where else to go. When you're homeless and penniless. When you don't have anything. That's why they call it the Young Strays. That's what I am."

"Don't you have parents?"

"No father, no mother, no brother . . . Nothing. Just my hands in my pockets." I laughed.

"You're quite a comic, you are."

"I don't have much choice."

I'd found out about the Young Strays through the Timone hospital, where I'd stayed for a month, being treated for second degree burns. Not only on my face, but all over my body. I'd traveled from Algiers to Marseilles in the machine room of a freighter called the *Nordland*. Hiding just over the pipes. When I came out, the guys in the crew were taken aback. Not because I was there, but because of the state I was in. "I'm thirsty," I said. That was all I could say before I passed out. When I came to, I was in the ER.

The doctors told me I'd been crazy to do a thing like that. They were right, but I'd gotten out of that fucking country, and I was still alive.

I told Rico the story. "One night, these twenty guys in fatigues and combat boots, with hoods over their heads, came to the project where I lived. In Bal-elzouar. They went into one block after another and pulled people out of their apartments. But not just anybody . . . They had lists. They ordered them down onto the street. Whole families. And then, pow, pow, pow . . . they shot them. My parents were on the list. My brother too."

Rico had his eyes closed. For a moment, I thought he'd fallen asleep, but when I stopped speaking, he opened his

eyes. I can't describe the look in them. It was like the look of
a blind man.

"And where were you?" he asked.

"By chance, I'd stayed over at my friend Zineb's place.
We'd gone bathing in the harbor. I always slept at his place
when we went bathing. Because it was too far for me to get
home from there. It's out near the airport, and . . . Anyway, I
liked sleeping at his place. My only regret is that I left Zineb
behind. In all that shit . . ."

Rico put his arm right down inside the cart, took out a bottle of cheap wine, and downed more than a quarter of it, just
like that, without drawing breath.

"Yes," he said, "it's always the same story."

"What's the same story?"

"You see, the thing is . . . You're living a quiet life with your
wife and kid. Just enough money not to be in the shit. And
then one day your wife dumps you. You find yourself alone.
You think it's the end of the world . . ."

His eyes glazed over. He was somewhere far away. For a
while, he was silent.

"What was I saying?"

"You were talking about your wife . . . The end of the
world."

"Oh, yes. In fact, the end of the world had already started.
Long before the hassles came along."

It was a lot of hot air, and I didn't understand any of it.
"What are you talking about?"

"It's when the sky falls on your head that you discover the
horror. The horror that exists in the world. Because suddenly
you're thrown into another life, and you meet people you never
even knew existed, whose pain you never knew existed . . ."

"Like me?"

"Like you. Others too, abandoned at the side of the road."
He took another big swig of wine, then went on, "You know,

it's like World War I. Did they teach you about World War I in school?"

"Are you kidding? My grandfather was in that war. As an infantryman. They even gave him a medal."

"Well, there was the front. The trenches. Men were dropping like flies. It was a slaughterhouse, that fucking war. And all the time, on both sides, life went on . . . It's just the same today. Except that the slaughterhouses are getting bigger. They're taking over the world. One day, you see, we'll all be dead."

He put the top back on the bottle and slipped it back inside the cart. He looked at me, with that look I liked. Then he nodded.

"So, shall we go down to the sea?"

20.

EVIL IS LIKE HELL, YOU CAN'T IMAGINE IT

The first thing Rico had done when he arrived in Marseilles was to climb to the top of Rue Neuve-Sainte-Catherine. To the little building where Léa used to live. The housefronts in the neighborhood, as in other parts of the center, had been repainted ocher and pink. He barely recognized the place.

That made him hesitate. Then he remembered the corridor, and the narrow staircase leading to her apartment. There, nothing had changed. The same light brown paint, but dirtier, of course.

"This is it," he said, when he took me there.

He'd wanted me to see where Léa's place was. We went back there several times. It was a kind of pilgrimage. It always took a hell of a long time to get there. Because it's all uphill. Rico would stop every hundred yards to catch his breath. He would always look at the names on the letter boxes. Just the way he'd done that first day in Marseilles.

Of course, he wasn't under any illusion that day. Twenty years had gone by. Maybe more. All the same, his heart was pounding as he read the names on the letter boxes. No Léa Carabédian. He'd read the names again, more slowly. To make absolutely sure.

Feeling lost, thinking of nothing, he had walked as far as the square in front of the Abbaye Saint-Victor. Leaning on the parapet that overlooks the former careening basin and the entrance to the Vieux-Port, he had looked out at the city and smoked one cigarette after another.

Marseilles, he told me—and I think it had surprised

him—had seemed familiar to him. As if he had lived here for years. More familiar than Saint-Brieuc, where he was born, and had grown up. More familiar than Rennes, where he had lived.

"Happiness tames everything, you know."

Rico said that one evening, when we were on our way back from Léa's.

"You want to repeat that?"

"Drop it, Abdou. Drop it."

Rico was like that a lot in those last weeks. We'd be talking about something or other, and then suddenly, in the middle of a sentence, in the middle of a word, his mind would wander. He'd be silent for a while, lost in thought. When he came out of it, he'd say some crazy phrase or other.

It annoyed me a little. I'd have liked to understand. I'd have liked him to explain.

"I'm not dumb, you know!" I'd yelled at him one day.

The fact is, Rico found it harder and harder to put the pieces together in his head. There was a big gap between what he was thinking and what he managed to express.

I'd noticed that when it came to Léa.

When he talked about her, he often got confused. The way he described her face, it was just how I'd pictured Mirjana. In his memory, their features had gotten all mixed up. The color of their eyes, their hair.

Rico had a serious problem with time. The notion of time. He couldn't imagine Léa the way she was now. A woman of forty. To him, she was still the same age as when they had met. Still young.

I tried to tell him that once, but it was no good.

I was waiting for him on the bench, on Place de Lenche. When I saw him come out from Rue Caisserie, I guessed that something had happened. He was walking quickly, pushing his cart any old how. He collapsed onto the bench, gasping for breath. I'd never seen him so excited.

"You're not going to believe this . . ." he began, and coughed.

"Wait, I said. "Catch your breath first."

"Yeah . . . yeah . . ."

I thought he was going to choke. I was always scared he would choke.

"I'm sure it was her. Léa . . ."

"Calm down, for fuck's sake!"

"Calm down? Shit, Abdou! I saw her! On a bus . . . She was getting on a bus. A No. 83. From the stop by the harbor, you know the one I mean? She even recognized me . . . I think so anyway. But it was too late. The bus was already leaving and—"

"What did she look like?"

"What do you mean, what did she look like?" He looked at me as if I was a moron.

"What about her face?"

"What do you mean, her face?"

Definitely a complete moron.

"You see, Rico . . ." I turned it over and over in my mind, and finally came out with it. "Let me explain something, Rico. Whatever we do, we change with time. Don't you understand that? We change. We get older. I'm sure if you pass me in the street in twenty years time, you won't recognize me."

Rico gave a shrill, rather crazy little laugh, which I didn't like. "Oh, yeah . . . In twenty years time . . ." He started coughing and retching, like when he was going to vomit. "In twenty years' time," he resumed, "I'll be dead. So don't talk crap, Abdou, about me not recognizing you . . . I'm not talking about you, I'm talking about Léa. Léa, who I just saw . . ."

Then there was that look in his eyes again, as if he was going under. Like the *Titanic* but speeded up. I was angry at myself for talking a lot of bullshit. They say it's better to keep quiet sometimes, don't they? What difference did it make, after all? As long as Rico believed he would see Léa again, he'd carry on living. And what did it matter if this Léa looked like Sophie, or Julie, or Malika, or Mirjana? Memories deceive us, I thought.

I even thought it out loud.

"What did you say?" he asked.

"Shit, man! I can talk crap too if I want to."

"Yeah . . ." He had lit himself a cigarette. The first drag made him cough again.

"I'm sorry," I said. "About Léa. I didn't mean to make you angry."

Rico shrugged, and his smile returned. "Guess what, Abdou? She was wearing that little red beret I liked . . . I told you about the beret, remember?"

I nodded. What was I supposed to say?

"I'm going to that bus stop tomorrow, and I'm going to wait for her." He put his arm around my shoulders and hugged me. There were tears in his eyes. "I'm going to surprise her!"

I let him talk. I knew that by the next morning he'd have forgotten. Not about Léa, but about Bus No. 83 and the stop by the harbor. It would only take a few beers, or a bottle of cheap wine, and a night's sleep, and everything would melt away in his head.

I'd come to terms with it. We didn't make appointments anymore, him and me. Because he always forgot them. Once, we'd arranged to meet outside a cheap clothing store almost at the bottom of Rue de la République. I hung about for two hours before I gave up. The easiest thing to do, I'd discovered, was to wait for him somewhere on his usual route. Either at the end of the sea wall by the Fort Saint-Jean. Or at his crash pad.

"Oh, there you are there," he'd say when he saw me, wherever the place, whatever the time. "I'm not too late . . ."

And he'd start telling these incredible stories, with past and present all mixed up. It hasn't been easy for me, I can tell you, trying to put everything in the right order.

Don't forget, he really took a beating in Avignon. Something must have gone off the rails inside his head, in my opinion. I'm not saying he was crazy, please don't think that. All I'm saying is that violence and pain traumatize you. When you've been beaten up, you're never the same again. You don't feel things in the same way. You don't react like other people.

I'm like that myself. Sometimes, even the most understanding people—I'm thinking of Michel, who works at the center as part of his military service—sometimes get irritated because they don't understand our reactions. Especially when they try to help us and we tell them to piss off.

The people at the center, the judges at juvenile court, all of those guys, however interested they are in what's happened to us, however moved, however indignant, it's impossible for them to put themselves in our skin. It's like with my burns. I just have to rub my face, and I'm not part of the same world anymore. This world. Evil is unreal. It's like hell. If you haven't been on the rack, you can't imagine it.

Even Driss doesn't understand. Driss also works at the center. He's a Moroccan, but he was born in Marseilles.

One day at the center, he cornered Karim and me. He wanted a word with us, he said. He sounded just like my teacher when I'd screwed up.

"I have a principle," he said. "I steer clear of anyone who touches dope."

That evening, I'd smoked so much dope, my eyes were as big as lottery balls. But it was Karim that Driss was particularly angry with. He turned to him and said, "I'm not talking to you anymore, O.K.? Not while you continue with that crap."

It's true that Karim was always smoking dope and taking anything he could find. He just wanted to get as high as possible. To be in another place. He's not a junkie, in my opinion. It's just that when he comes back down to earth, the first thing that comes into his mind is those three fucking soldiers beating his mother. To force her to inform on a neighbor. In the end, it was Karim who informed on him. He couldn't bear to hear his mother screaming anymore. So those bastards went and got the neighbour and shot him in front of Karim. Three bullets. One each. Blood spattered over Karim's shirt. That's always in his mind too—his neighbor's blood spurting over him.

Karim shrugged. He really didn't give a shit if Driss stopped speaking to him. He gave us both the finger and took off. It was the cops who brought him back, five days later. "We found one of your protégés," they said, laughing. To them, the Young Strays was just a den of junkies.

I felt bad for Karim, seeing him come back like that, flanked by the cops. Bad for Driss too. You can't just stop speaking to someone like that, I thought. So, one morning, I just lost it. I waited until Christine, the secretary of the center, went to the toilet, and then I took her place behind the desk.

When she came back, I said to her, in a serious voice, "Sit down, mademoiselle."

Christine smiled, as she always does. With that pretty smile of hers, which calms us down and makes us think that everyone at the center really cares about us.

"So, Christine," I said, "how did you get to France? What was the name of the boat?"

The others came closer. Michel and Driss first of all. And then the others like me. Karim, Faisal, Mario, Nedim, Hiner . . . They were all laughing.

Christine played along with me, until I went a little too far, past the point of no return.

"Oh, so it wasn't a boat, it was a truck? . . . Eighteen hundred miles, hidden under a truck. I see . . . All the way from Kurdistan? My God."

Hiner came closer. That was what he'd lived through. He'd swallowed the whole of this crappy life on the road. For eighteen hundred miles.

I looked Christine straight in the eyes, and said, very solemnly, "Ah, so there's poverty in your country . . ."

That was when she cut me off. She'd stopped smiling.

"All right," she said. "That's enough, Abdou. I have work to do."

The telephone was ringing, so that much was true.

And it was true she was up to her ears in work. Because of us. Us young strays were always creating lots of paperwork.

And not all my ideas are good ones.

The only reason I'm talking about myself is to explain. So that you get a better idea of things. Those fucking pimps had left Rico for dead. He had no idea how long he'd stayed there like that. Two days, three days. Maybe more. As soon as he had regained consciousness the first time, he had dragged himself to the mattress, and then everything had gone black again.

And in the blackness was the horror. The blows started raining down again. Endlessly. On his back, his stomach, his face. He hurt so much, he couldn't feel his body anymore. He hurt so much, he wanted to scream. And in his head, a bell kept ringing, like in a boxing ring. One knockout blow after another.

What really woke him was the cough. And the desire to throw up. Thick, yellowish phlegm, mixed with a little blood. He had spat it out on the floor, without getting up. Every time he coughed, it seemed to rip his stomach apart. It was only gradually that he had realized he was stinking of shit and piss. He'd done it in his clothes. Not in his sleep, but while those scumbags were beating him up. Or just after. His whole body had let go. With the fear, and the pain.

At some point, he had crawled to his rucksack, and had taken a whole strip of Dolipran and washed it down with the only beer he had left. Then he had fallen asleep again.

"Mirjana!"

He had woken with a start, feeling anxious. Without getting up off the floor, he had looked around the room. Searching for the book of poems. He had been reading it when those guys had arrived. So the book should have been against the wall. It wasn't there. Rico was relieved. She had taken it with her.

She would live.

"Mirjana," he had whispered.

And he had fallen asleep again with a smile.

When he had finally seen his face in a mirror, he'd had a fright. His whole face was swollen. His right eye, his cheek. His nose. And his lips, which had doubled in size, were split in several places.

It was in that state that he had arrived in Marseilles.

If Léa had been there, waiting for him, she would obviously have taken him in her arms and consoled him, looked after him, pampered him.

"I love you," she would have said.

But Léa wasn't there.

Only soldiers in fatigues with submachine guns in their hands, patrolling among the travelers. A whole bunch of riot police too.

A city at war, Rico had thought.

Sarajevo.

But it was only Marseilles.

It was Marseilles.

"I'm here, Titi," he had muttered, threading his way through the crowd to avoid the soldiers and the cops.

Marseilles.

The end of the road. His road.

He had left the station. To his right, he had seen three dropouts propped against a wall, apparently having an afternoon nap. He had slumped against the wall, next to one of them.

"Hi," he had said. "Do you know a shelter where I could spend the night?"

21.

ONE DAY, MAYBE, I'LL DISCOVER BROTHERS

Rico's crash pad was not far from the harbor of la Joliette. A few hundred yards from the harbor station, on Quai de la Tourette. A gloomy place, scheduled for redevelopment. The disused warehouses were all boarded up to deter squatters, and their walls were covered in posters, tags and obscene graffiti.

Rico had spent so long hanging around the docks, he'd finally found a way in other than by the street. A real stroke of luck.

Late one afternoon, he took me there. We had been inseparable for two weeks.

"You'll see . . . You'll see . . ." he kept saying as we walked.

He was really happy. I wanted to hold his hand, the way I used to hold my father's hand, but I didn't dare.

From Place de Lenche, we turned onto Rue de l'Évêché, and walked as far as the cathedral of La Major. A heavy building caked with grime, shaped like a rum baba, surrounded by the road leading to the coast highway. We went all the way around the outside of it.

"That," Rico said with a laugh, "is Place de l'Esplanade."

I could see why he was laughing. The square had disappeared under the four-lane road. There were lots of cars, going as fast as if they were on a racing circuit.

"How do we cross?"

"Easy. We just cross." He pointed to the white stripes on the asphalt. "We're within our rights, there's a pedestrian crossing."

Rico raised his left arm, like a cop, and set off, pushing his cart in front of him. I followed, with my eyes closed. There was

188 of JEAN-CLAUDE IZZO

a lot of furious braking, and hooting of horns, but we got to the other side in one piece.

"It's like everything else, you mustn't be afraid. Mirjana used to say that."

We were at the top of a broad flight of steps leading to a street. Rue François-Moisson. I always came that way, later. I didn't want to be knocked down by a car. I was too young to die.

"We could have come from down there."

"True. But I prefer not to climb."

We went down the steps until we reached the first terrace. On the left, in a recess, there was a low, rusty door, which led to a narrow gallery. The stench was amazing. Like centuries of cat's piss and dogshit.

"Are you O.K.?" Rico asked, seeing me pull a face.

"You don't have a gas mask, do you?"

"It gets better, you'll see."

He picked up a big torch from where it lay hidden behind a parpen, and we walked more than five hundred yards on uneven ground.

In fact, the stench came from a pipe that ran along the side of the gallery. A sewer pipe, I guess. I realized now the source of the smell Rico carried around with him, an acrid smell, a mixture of decay and damp. I'd thought at first it was just because he was dirty. He was so impregnated with it, you could even smell it on his breath sometimes.

"This place must be infested with rats," I said.

"I don't know about rats. A rat, yes."

"What do you mean, a rat?"

"I mean, a rat. There's one who comes to see me regularly. We're pals. If I wake up at night, I see his red eyes. He watches over me."

I shuddered. I hate rats. They give me the creeps. Ever since I travelled on that fucking freighter. The machine room was full of them. And the noise they made! Squealing. Crawling over each other. I had felt the fucking things crawling over me too.

"Oh, yeah?" I said ironically. "So what do you do, feed him?"

"I told you, we're pals. I talk to him, and I feed him. You won't believe this, but he loves sausage. He sits down on his hind paws . . ." He stopped to describe the scene, even imitating the rat. " . . . and he holds the slice in his little front paws and gobbles it down. It's so funny."

I thought of the times I used to watch Tom and Jerry on TV with Zineb. "And does he have a little towel to wipe his face?" I joked.

Rico shone his torch in my face. "What has that rat ever done to you?"

"Nothing . . . Nothing . . ."

"Then don't be nasty to him, dammit."

We came to an openwork wooden door. This was where Rico had settled in. It was what we call a *fundouk* in Algiers.

"The rats and I are almost the same family now."

He opened the door, then lit two big candles he'd filched from the church of Saint-Ferréol on Quai des Belges.

"Not bad, eh?"

It was a shock, I can tell you!

His crash pad was like Ali Baba's cave. There must have been at least two or three hundred plastic bags, filled to the brim with all sorts of objects. Everything neatly sorted. The books with the books, the knick-knacks with the knick-knacks, the clothes with the clothes . . . And all the bags divided into groups according to their contents.

I let out a whistle. "Shit! What do you do with all this?"

"I earn my living, what do you think?"

Rico had had enough of begging. Even after going over and over Titi's advice in his head. It really turned his stomach, he said. So he'd invented a system. If someone gave him a coin, he'd offer a gift in return.

"And does it work?"

He shrugged. "There's a bit of hustling involved. You see, the guy or the woman . . . they slip you a coin out of . . . compassion. They've just been shopping and they feel a little guilty because they have food to eat, clothes to wear, and so on . . . But it's never more than a few coins. With my system I can get between five and ten francs out of them! Minimum!"

Every day he would set up at the entrance to the Bourse Center, near the Canebière. A three-storey shopping mall. Rico would lay out a few books and objects on a clean sheet of newspaper and get to work.

He went up to people, more or less the way he had seen Titi doing it at the Aligre market. But confidently, without trying to make them feel sorry for him. "Hey Isabelle, you wouldn't have a little something for me? Hey, Jeannot, nothing for me today?" Rico called everyone Isabelle and Jeannot.

I went to see him "at work" one day. As soon as someone slipped him a coin, he'd take the person by the arm and draw him over to his display.

"Wait, come here, I'm going to give you a little gift. What would you like? The pink china cat? A book? The baseball cap? You choose . . ."

The person was trapped. Even if he said no, he'd end up with something and be forced to say thank you to Rico. And then Rico would open his hand and say with a smile, "Hold on, Jeannot, you're three francs short. The book costs five francs."

That threw people.

"Well, I don't know if I have three francs," the "customer" would say.

And he would start searching his pockets, looking in his wallet. It would never even occur to him to give his "gift" back to Rico.

Rico had an eagle eye. "Isn't that ten francs you have there?" he'd ask.

"Oh, yes," the other person would say.

"Here, I'll give you back your two francs, and we're fine. O.K.?"

Only then did Rico say thank you, have a nice day, that kind of thing. Always remembering to compliment the women. "You're a cute one, Isabelle." "You have a lovely wife, Jeannot."

I never saw anyone tell him to piss off with his gifts. I think people enjoyed his trickery. I even saw a guy shake his hand once. Rico had just given him a book with a blue cover. *Spelling Course* by E. and Madame Bled.

"It's extremely rare," he said.

"Come back some time, Jeannot. I have plenty more. Real collector's items . . ."

Rico emptied his cart, and started sifting through the things he'd picked up during the day.

I collapsed onto an old mattress wedged between the bags of books. The teddy bear was there, propped against a wall.

"Hello, Zineb," I murmured.

I don't know if Rico heard me or what, but he turned and scowled at me. "You're still after that bear!"

"Shit, Rico! I can say hello to him, can't I?"

"Yeah, yeah, O.K. . . ."

I caught sight of a bicycle at the far end of the room. "What's that bike?"

"Just a bike."

Rico was grouchy. Because of Zineb. I mean, because of the bear.

"Come on," I said, standing up. "Don't make a face."

"It was lying at the bottom of the steps for a week. Haven't you ever had a bike either?"

We looked at each other. The dickhead was really sulking. I didn't understand why he was so upset about that bear.

"Yes," I replied, gently. "Well, my brother did. I like cycling . . . Does it work?"

"Yes . . . I pushed it along the street. Just to see. It runs smoothly enough. I mean, you wouldn't win the Tour de France with it."

"Well . . ."

"I always dreamed of having one. I'd have liked to ride along the beach on Sunday, with Sophie and Julien. But Sophie . . ."

He went and sat down on the mattress to smoke a cigarette. I joined him. He picked up the bear and sat it down between his legs.

"The thing is, it reminds me of my son, this bear. I bought him one once that looked a bit like that. He never let it out of his sight. I wonder if he still has it."

"Why shouldn't he still have it?"

"Who knows? There are many things we don't understand . . ." He looked at me, with that tender look that did me so much good. "At night, I hug the bear. I tell myself it brings me a little closer to my son."

"You miss him, huh?" I said, stupidly.

"I miss everything, Abdou. But I don't want anything. Can you explain that? I don't even want to see him, or give him a hug, or kiss him."

I felt like crying, dammit.

"But maybe he wants it. It's like with me and my folks . . ."

I started bawling.

I'd just remembered them, for the first time since that fucking night. It was July 5th. National Independence Day. The streets were swarming with people. My father was holding my hand. My mother was walking beside him. We were looking for a taxi. He had promised to take us to Sidi Ferruch, a beautiful beach about nine miles from Algiers.

I was happy.

There were lots of happy days, in that country.

On the way back, I remember, the radio in the taxi had announced that a bomb had just gone off in the market at Baradi, fifteen miles away. As if nothing had happened, the driver put on a cassette. By Cheb Mami, my favourite singer.

Ayit fik en'ssaaf ouanti m'aamda
Li bik biya oua Alache sada

Disaster didn't exist.
It was still a long way away.

Alche Alache Alache Ya lile
Alche Alache Alache Ya ain
Alche Alache Alache . . .

Rico drew me to him. "We can't do anything about these things, Abdou. It's as if life has gotten out of control, and . . . No, not life . . . Evil. I don't know why. Titi didn't know. Or Félix. Or Mirjana. Maybe you'll know, one day . . ."

I sniffed, then wiped my tears. "You think, one day . . ."

"Maybe, maybe . . . when millions of people are dead. Wait . . ."

He lifted his head and took a book from under the mattress. *The Odyssey* by Homer. A piece of paper was sticking out.

"I found this in a book. Not this one, another one. Here, read it."

The handwriting was beautiful. Big and round. A girl's handwriting, I thought. *Perhaps when millions of people have been destroyed, others will be created, and I will discover brothers where I thought I had none.*

"That's a bit preachy, isn't it?"

"It may explain a few things . . ."

"Maybe . . . I think we all get taken in by words. It's like with the judge at juvenile court. He says he's only there to help you, says it bold as brass. At first, you think he's being good to you. But as soon as you think about it a little, as soon as you read between the lines, you realize he's going to send you back to your country when you're eighteen. Whether you like it or not."

"I don't know, Abdou. All those things . . . I don't know anymore. You see . . ." Suddenly, a grave look came over his face and he pointed at my burns. "Does that hurt?" he asked.

He almost put his hand on my cheek. But he didn't. His fingers simply traced the scars in the air. The way he had traced the ass of the girl in the poster. With the same tenderness.

With love.

It was the first time someone had dared ask me that question. If anyone else had done it, even at the center, I'd have punched him in the face for sure.

"Yes, sometimes. I have to be careful it doesn't get infected."

"You can have the bear, if you like." And he thrust it at me.

"No kidding?"

"Do I look as if I'm kidding?"

"You're great!"

Our eyes met.

"I think I'll leave him here. What do you say? He's fine here. And anyway . . . I can come and see him whenever I like, right?"

"That's O.K. by me."

We looked at each other again.

"I'll call him Zineb. Do you mind?"

"Is that your friend who stayed down there?"

I nodded.

"Hello, Zineb," Rico said.

22.

HOURS AND HOURS SPENT LOOKING AT THE SEA

While all this was happening, I didn't spend much time at the Young Strays, as you can imagine. I'd go there in the morning and again in the evening, to sign the register. Just to make sure I had my board and lodging!

They'd accepted it at the center. As the judge had said, I'm not easy to control.

A refusenik, that's what I am.

I refuse to accept what happened to me. I'll never accept it. I don't want to.

The important thing, Driss had told me, is that I keep in contact. He was worried about me. About Karim too. And all the kids who ended up at the center.

"Don't go kidding yourself, Abdou," he had said to me when I arrived from the hospital. "There's no future here, as far as a job and papers go."

I'd liked him for saying that. At least, the situation was clear. The future wasn't here, or at home. Or anywhere else.

And at any moment, you can screw up. Become a dealer. Attack an old lady. Hold up a drugstore. You just have to get the idea in your head, and not be able to find a reason not to do it.

I realized that one afternoon when I saw the latest Nikes, in Go Sport. Just looking at them gave me cramps in my stomach. Like when you're hungry. Why can't I afford them? Why can others afford them and not me? What did I ever do to the Prophet? All these questions come into your mind. And only one answer. That life's unfair. And that's how it begins.

Driss and I talked about this quite a lot. In Arabic. I only mention that, because at the center they prefer us to talk French. On the wall when you come in there's a sign that says: *He who speaks the language of the people averts disaster.* But it does me good to speak my own language, at least to say those things that keep going through my head. I can express them better. And understand myself better too.

"And besides, there's Rico," I'd said to Driss. "I can't just abandon him. You look after me, I look after him . . . He's going to die."

"Listen, we can help him."

That was what they'd told Rico at the shelter on Rue Forbin. They could help him. Take care of him.

"Help me do what?" he'd asked.

"To get you away from all this. Find you a job. We've done it for others. You don't want to be like this for the rest of your days, do you?"

"Why not?"

"Rico, this isn't a life. You know that."

"What *is* a life? That?" He had pointed to a guy in a suit who was rushing past them with a cellphone pressed to his ear. "I've already had that life. I know where it leads. Exactly where I am today. So stop bugging me, Jeannot."

And he'd burned his bridges. He'd had nothing more to do with any of the centers and shelters. At the beginning, while he was searching for a crash pad, he'd even slept in containers down in the harbor.

Rico would never be in the statistics for rehabilitation. Others would. Fortunately for them. Or unfortunately, I'm not sure anymore. But for every one who escaped that life, how many were going under at that very same moment? Driss and I had talked about that too. He hadn't been able to give me an answer. Or tell me how many people there were on the street in Marseilles, like Rico. A thousand? Two thousand? Or how many young illegals there were like me. There were a hundred eighty on the register at the Young Strays alone . . .

"Him and me, we're the lucky ones," I'd said to Driss.

He had blown his top at that. "Shit, Abdou! There's a medical service specially for people like him. I mean, you're not stupid. They can look after him. You say he's your friend . . ."

I felt as if I was hearing Rico trying to persuade Titi to go to hospital. I didn't want Rico to avoid me, refuse to speak to me, as Titi had done with him. I accepted him the way he was. I was trying to understand him. I wanted to be with him to the end. And I felt bad about it. Shit, you can understand that, can't you?

"Stop, Driss! That's not what Rico wants."

He'd gotten really annoyed. "No one can want to die."

I'd looked at him. My big brother in Marseilles. We weren't always on the same wavelength. It's as if we were on different sides, not enemies exactly, but . . . strangers, even though we spoke the same language. Why?

"I often do," I'd said. "In the morning, when I open my eyes."

"Stop talking crap, Abdou!"

I'd stopped, of course. I'd done my usual patented about-turn. Like: Don't worry, Driss, the only thing I care about is smoking dope. I really have a ball. Where there's grass, there's hope . . . Then I went and gave Christine a kiss and set off to look for Rico.

My day was just beginning.

The best moment of the day was when Rico and I went down to the sea. Whatever the weather, unless it was pouring with rain. First we dropped by his crash pad. He'd empty his cart, sift through everything and put it away, then take a strip of Dolipran with a little wine or beer, and we'd set off, going as far as the end of the sea wall by the Fort Saint-Jean. Cutting across the wharves, where they'd knocked down the old warehouses.

We liked it there. At the entrance to the channel. Facing the Sainte-Marie lighthouse, on the other, bigger sea wall.

"When the weather's good, I'll take you to the other side. Up the lighthouse. You see the staircase there, on the left? You can climb up, and when you get to the top, you can sit down with your back against the stone and look out at the sea and the islands. It's fantastic. It's the most beautiful thing I've ever seen in my life."

Léa had taken him there. At her school, she'd managed to get a Port Authority permit to take photos. What she'd really wanted to do was watch the sun go down over the harbor with Rico.

They had made love up there, on the platform of the lighthouse.

Often, when he looked at the sea, fragments of memory would come back to him, and time would fall back into place in his head.

Rico was staring at the lighthouse. "Léa . . ."

She had unbuttoned his fly, then had lifted her dress and come and sat down astride him. Her body pressed to his. Burning hot. They had stayed like that, clasped in an embrace, looking into each other's eyes, for an eternity.

Her lips had brushed his, leaving a salt taste on them, then moved over his cheek to his neck, his ear, titillating the lobe, then returned to his face. To his half-open mouth, which was waiting for her kiss. Her tongue.

"Don't move," she had murmured.

Rico had been in an agony of excitement.

"Don't move."

Her legs had held his waist, like clinging seaweed, and she had started to move imperceptibly, her hands clutching his shoulders. Her tanned skin bathed in the setting sun and wet with salty sea spray.

"Joining our destinies," Rico murmured, still staring at the lighthouse.

"What?" I asked.

"I think she said that. Something about joining our destinies to the sea. I can't remember."

As often happened when he was making an effort to remember, Rico was tiring himself out. He put his hands together in front of him, as if to pray.

"She loved the sea. This sea. She taught me to love it. By linking our desires to it, I think. She used to say . . . that it was . . . that it was like a dream, that's it. That this sea is like a dream you must look at with your eyes open, a dream you wouldn't wake from. Do you understand that?"

I nodded.

I didn't really understand, but I sensed what it meant, and that was O.K. by me.

"You can always be wrong," Rico said laconically, lighting a cigarette.

"Do you mind explaining that? I don't follow you."

"Doesn't matter . . ." He puffed ferociously at his cigarette, then took the book from his pocket. *The Odyssey*. That book, he had told me, reminded him of Léa. For some time now I'd been reading it to him. Rico couldn't concentrate anymore on the words and sentences. I didn't mind, and anyway it was a good story.

"Here, read."

At first, Rico had lost his temper a lot because I asked a lot of questions, every time I came across a name I didn't know.

"What's a nymph?" I'd asked.

"For fuck's sake, Abdou, don't stop on every word! What does it matter what a nymph is? Her name is Calypso, right? And she's a nymph, right? . . . What matters is the story, dammit! The music of the story. If we have to know and understand everything, we'll soon get pissed off . . . O.K.? Now start again from the beginning."

"*Now only he still desired to return to his wife, for an august*

nymph held him captive deep in her caverns, Calypso, that divine
being who longed to have him as her husband."

We could spend hours like that, not talking. Sitting side by
side. Until the dampness of evening woke us from our torpor.
Rico would smoke one cigarette after another, absently, and I
would watch him. He seemed to be letting go, moving into
something I found incomprehensible. Sometimes, a smile
would appear on his lips, a smile that made me shudder.

"Why are you smiling?" I asked.

That was two days before all this.

"I'm smiling about my dream, if you must know. Shit, can't
you just keep quiet for a minute?"

I felt the cold that was in him settle in me.

He wasn't dreaming about Léa. He wasn't dreaming about
Mirjana. I knew that. He was dreaming about the faceless
woman with the soft, caressing voice. The one who came to
him more and more frequently at night, took his hand and
asked, "Why aren't you smiling? Why won't you give me a
smile?"

I wanted to get up and run through the streets of Marseilles,
to look for Léa. Shit, there must be a Léa somewhere! A Léa
who could say to him, "It's me, Rico. I've waited so long, if
only you knew . . ." A Léa who would give flesh to his memories, to the hopes of his youth. And would finally get the
thoughts in his head into some kind of order. Once and for all!

I could see it, dammit! I could just see it.

The world would get back on course.

Back in the right direction.

The direction of life.

Bullshit!

I wanted Rico to take me in his arms. And say to me, "I love
you, son." The way my father used to, when I went to bed. Just
to help me believe, before I went to sleep, that there'd be a

tomorrow, that there'd be celebrations, and barbecues, and Tom and Jerry on TV, and soccer matches, and endless swims in the harbor, and girls to look at . . .

"I'm freezing here," I said, standing up.

"I'm coming," Rico replied.

I had the impression he wasn't there anymore. That he'd already gone.

I walked with my hands in my pockets. An old Algerian was fishing. I had noticed him as we were coming. He'd been there at least two hours, and I hadn't seen him catch a single thing.

"Are they biting?" I asked in French.

"*Meïtta*," he replied in Arabic.

It's dead here.

Another angler had told Zineb and me the same thing, last summer, in the harbor of Algiers.

Meïtta.

Léa, I think, had said to Rico, "Looking at the sea, you know, I understand how much life I have in me. There's nothing on land. The land is ugly. Nothing changes there. It's as if everything is dead. Even the people . . ."

But it might have been Mirjana who had said that.

Or Rico who had muttered it one evening.

Or maybe I'd thought it myself.

Because I did think it.

23.

A LITTLE CAR RIDE ON RUE SAINTE-FRANÇOISE

I was sitting on the old mattress, waiting for Rico. I'd been waiting for hours.

"What do you think, Zineb?" I asked the teddy bear.

He didn't think anything, so we just kept on waiting.

I hadn't seen Rico all day. I'd been up and down his usual route twice, without success. The Bourse Center, the church of Saint-Ferréol, Quai du Port, Rue Caisserie, Place de Lenche, Quai du Fort Saint-Jean. Checking his crash pad each time.

I was in a foul mood from not knowing where he was. Something must have happened to make him change his routine.

Something major.

The second time I checked his crash pad, his cart was there. But the things he'd collected hadn't been sorted. Beside the cart, a large, worn canvas sailor's bag.

He'd met someone.

I rolled a huge joint, and smoked it slowly. I'd gotten it from Karim. It was Colombian. "The best, you'll see."

I love that moment when I take the first drag, and the smoke hits the back of my throat. Closing my eyes and holding my breath, I feel it take me over. I release it slowly, just as my temples start to throb. It's so good.

It would have been nicer still if I'd had some cute chick with me. The girl in the *Aubade* poster, for example. Salima, she'd be called. No, not Salima! Are you crazy or what, Abdou? Have you ever seen an Arab woman showing her ass like that? No. Marina, then. Not bad, sounds Italian. Or Carmen. No, not Carmen . . .

I looked at Zineb, and blew a little smoke at his head. Smell that, Zineb? That's good grass. Real fucking good.

Vanessa. That's it. Vanessa. With tits like Sophie Marceau.

"Give me a drag," she'd say, tugging at her little lace panties.

She'd stay like that, keeping the pose she had on the poster. All the time. Well, for a while, anyway. Until the whole of Lesson 27 was over. I'd put my dry lips against hers and, just as Mirjana had done to Rico, I'd release the smoke in her throat.

"Like it, Vanessa?"

Of course she'd like it.

My brother used to say it was good for girls to smoke a little dope before fucking. It made their bodies softer, more pliable, like you couldn't imagine.

No, I couldn't imagine. I still can't. I still haven't slept with a girl. But after a few drags of that Colombian, Vanessa would of course be as soft and pliable as *khobz-al-aid*, the feast-day bread my mother used to bake.

Wow . . . Vanessa . . .

I stubbed out the butt. I had a hard on like a Moroccan mule. Zineb couldn't get over it. I grabbed my burning dick. It was all prickly inside, as if it was full of hot sauce. *Dersa*.

Fucking Colombian!

Vanessa.

I fell asleep.

I was woken by voices in the gallery. I leaped to my feet. Shit, with all that had happened, I'd forgotten to go to the center and sign the register. Driss was going to bawl me out. The voices came closer.

Rico came in.

There was a guy behind him. Rico was holding two big pizza boxes and a plastic bag with bottles clinking inside it. The guy was carrying four more large bags.

"This is Dédé!" Rico cried, extremely excited. "Dédé, can you imagine? Fucking bozo's been in Marseilles for four days already!"

"Hi," Dédé said.

"I'm Abdou."

"I know."

"Put everything down on the mattress," Rico said.

There were two twelve-packs of beer, six bottles of wine and a half-bottle of whisky.

"We're going to have a party," Rico announced.

"It stinks in here," Dédé said, lighting a cigarette.

"Where the hell were you?" I asked. "I've been looking all over."

"We went for a few drinks," Dédé replied. "I've been looking for this jerk for four days! I've been everywhere. The night shelter on Rue Forbin, the Madrague-Ville hostel, the drop-in center on Place Marceau. It was like a treasure hunt. Everywhere I went, I found someone who thought he'd seen him . . ."

"In the end we just bumped into each other," Rico said. "On the Vieux-Port. We came back here, and then we went out again to catch up with everything . . . Shit, a whole year . . . Hey, guess what? They released Jo! That was . . . how long ago did you say?"

"Six months."

"Right, six months. And wait for this. Apart from all the apologies, he's really hit the jackpot. 2,600 francs in compensation for every day he spent in the can! Just think of that, Abdou. That's adds up to quite a sum."

"If they'd given Jo a life sentence," Dédé joked, "he'd be a millionaire!"

"How about Félix?" I asked.

Dédé shrugged.

"He's vanished," Rico said. "One morning, he was just gone. The only thing he took with him was his ball."

"I thought he'd have come down to Marseilles. He was always talking about it. And about you . . ."

"Apparently, Norbert, his boss, found him sleeping with his wife, Anne . . ."

"That's what they say anyway," Dédé said.

"And what does Norbert say?"

"How the hell should I know? Can you see me going to the farm and asking Norbert, 'So, man, is it true that Félix fucked your wife?'" Dédé laughed as if he'd just told a dirty joke.

"I don't believe it," Rico said. "I can't imagine Félix doing that."

I couldn't imagine it either.

From what Rico had told me about Félix, it didn't seem like the kind of thing he'd do. There must have been some kind of quarrel between Dédé and Félix, I thought. Over Jo. Jo and Monique. Félix couldn't have approved of what Dédé had been doing.

"Why are you looking at me like that, boy?"

"No reason," I said. "No reason."

I didn't like the look of Dédé. I didn't think we were going to be friends, him and me. Rico had never told me what he thought of him, but in my opinion, a pal who fucks your girl while you're in the can is a real scumbag.

I couldn't stop thinking about it while I ate my slice of pizza.

Poor Félix. I'd have liked it if he'd ended up here. "I'd rather not talk about it," he'd have said. For sure.

"We haven't told you yet," Rico began.

After drinking a few *pastis* in a café on Grand'Rue, the two of them didn't even have a hundred francs left between them.

"We'll have to do something to get back on our feet again," Dédé had said.

"I'm too old for that now, Dédé. If things go bad, I can't run. I'd get nabbed in no time."

But Dédé had finally managed to persuade Rico. I don't think he'd needed much persuading. Listening to Rico telling me about their adventure, it was obvious he hadn't been able to resist the pleasure—and I mean pleasure—of scaring himself. Of playing the thief. One last time. You see, there wasn't a shred of violence in him. Nor a shred of hatred or nastiness, in spite of all he'd been through. Holdups weren't his thing. He was a good man, and always had been.

Dédé had done quite a bit of walking in the center of town and had spotted a good ATM machine on Place Sadi-Carnot. On Rue de la République, halfway between the Vieux-Port and La Joliette.

"After eight o'clock there's hardly anyone around. But lots of guys pull up in cars. And they don't waste their time looking for a parking space . . . You just have to be patient . . . As usual."

It was exactly eight by the Tax Office clock when they took up position near the bank. They sat down on the steps in front of an apartment building, a fifth of a gallon of wine in front of them, and smoked as they waited.

"A couple of bums aren't going to worry anyone," Dédé said. "It's actually reassuring."

After just fifteen minutes, they were approached by two black guys, who had been hanging around on the sidewalk for a while.

"Hey, you guys!" one of them growled, "go sleep it off somewhere else. We're working here! And you two stick out like a sore thumb."

"Just take off, O.K.?" the other one said.

"O.K., O.K.," Dédé moaned.

They stood up and shuffled across the street.

"That's it, Dédé. That ATM must be in the Michelin guide!"

"Piss artists!"

"No, we're doing O.K."

At that moment, a car stopped, a black Renault Clio. Dédé and Rico sat down, curious to see how the black guys would go about it. A girl, a brunette with glasses, was at the wheel. The man, a puny-looking young guy in a leather jacket, walked calmly toward the ATM.

"Shit, those two would have been perfect for us!"

In an instant, the black guys had come up behind the young guy. He turned around, with a huge gun in his hand.

"Police!" he yelled. "Don't move!"

The other black guy took off.

"Police!" the lady cop cried behind him. "Stay where you are!"

At that moment, a siren echoed on the street, and a police car arrived, cornering the fugitive.

Rico and Dédé almost felt like applauding.

"Better than a TV show," Rico said with a laugh.

"Yeah, the cops here are really good."

Rico stood up. "That bank must be in the police Michelin too!" He knocked back a swig of wine, watched the cops driving away, then passed the bottle to Dédé. "Well, now we just have to go home, like the idiots we are."

"Are you kidding? This is perfect!"

"Perfect how?"

"The cops aren't going to come by twice. Those two assholes must have been working this patch for a while, so obviously they got picked up. We're just passing through, right?"

"Dédé, you're completely crazy!"

"No, I'm thirsty. It'll be fine, trust me."

And they went back to their places near the ATM, the bottle of wine in front of them. Three cars stopped. A guy. Another guy. Then a guy and a girl.

Rico sighed. "There won't be anything left."

He was starting to feel tired. I don't think he was enjoying the game anymore.

"That one," Dédé said suddenly.

It was a brand new white Opel. With a couple inside.

"Keep cool, Rico. And we do what we agreed, O.K.?"

Rico nodded.

A young woman got out. A blonde. Her ass in a pair of tight-fitting black jeans. She left the car door open. Rico and Dédé approached.

"Have you got a hundred francs?" Dédé asked the young woman.

"No," she replied curtly.

Rico got in the car. "My pal has a knife. And he's crazy. If you move, if you scream, you can say goodbye to your Swedish girlfriend."

The man was the handsome older guy type, with silver temples and a small mustache. Lots of rings on his fingers. His hands on the wheel were shaking.

"Bingo!" Dédé cried.

He opened the rear door and pushed the girl inside. The smell of lavender filled the car.

"We live just around the corner," Dédé said. "Tell monsieur the way."

"Let us go," the guy whined.

"It isn't far," Rico said. "Do you know Rue Sainte-Françoise?"

He shook his head.

"No, I don't suppose it's a neighborhood you spend much time in. Go on, I'll direct you."

On Rue de l'Évêché, they drove past the police station.

"That's the cop house," Rico joked, "but they're not expecting us this evening."

On Place des Treize-Cantons, at the top of Rue Sainte-Françoise, Rico asked the guy to turn right. Onto a very narrow, one-way street. Rue du Petit-Puis. He was so freaked out, it took him two attempts to turn the corner.

"Stop," Rico said. "This is where we get off. You keep straight on. Without stopping. After this, it's downhill all the way, until you get back to civilization."

The guy drove off without asking any questions. Without even letting his chick get back in the front seat. Rico and Dédé took the steps behind them to get back to Rue de l'Évêché. Then they walked nice and slowly to Place de la Joliette. The pizza stand could have been waiting specially for them. As for the Chinese grocery, it was open day and night.

They'd gotten through four bottles of wine during the story. Two each. I was on beer. But I was taking it easy. Although I'd slept, the effects of the joint hadn't worn off. I was still numb. I still felt as if I was floating.

My nose felt itchy.

"What do you say?" Rico asked me.

"There are some Nikes at Go Sport," I drawled. "They're fantastic. Maybe I can have a little something."

My nose really itched.

When it came down to it, I preferred the company of Vanessa. My beautiful Colombian.

24.

SOMETIMES, LIFE IS REALLY MORE BEAUTIFUL
THAN DREAMS

They were singing at the tops of their voices. Especially Dédé, who sang in a loud, solemn voice. Rico was coughing fit to burst. A cough he tried to soothe with little gulps of whisky. They'd obviously finished the last two bottles of wine during my nap.

They were laughing and shouting out the names of songs, challenging each other. Often they only remembered the chorus, which they sang quickly before moving on to the next one.

What about this one by Charles Aznavour?

Or this one by Jacques Brel?

"*Jeff*," Dédé said. "Do you remember *Jeff*? Titi really liked that one!"

"Cheers, Titi!"

No, Jeff, you're not alone . . .

"Those fucking bastards, when I think about it . . ."

"Drop it, Dédé, please . . ."

I'd been watching them for a few minutes, lying on the mattress. I didn't like the way Dédé sang. He shouted, as if the words didn't mean anything.

"What about this one by Julien Clerc?" Rico said.

You don't like it, I know, that she's mine
But she's . . .

And Dédé screamed:

Mine, all mine . . .

I sat up slowly. My head was like the base for a squadron of helicopters! The blades turned and turned, and the din was incredible.

"You're making a hell of a lot of noise!"

"*We're having a party, having a party,*" Dédé sang.

"Are you all right?" Rico asked me.

He held out the bottle of whisky. I refused, making a face. I'd have happily drunk Niagara Falls. My mouth felt thick and coated, and my tongue must have trebled in size.

"What about this one?" Dédé said.

The girl from Cadiz has those velvety eyes . . .

Rico took it up. "*The girl from Cadiz, da-da-dum, da-da-dum.*"

"Shit, man! Luis Mariano! That's all we listened to in my house! Every fucking Sunday! Georges Guétary . . . and that woman . . . What was her name? Gloria Lasso, that was it. Gloria Lasso."

"I think I'd have preferred that. My dad was more into Strauss waltzes, strings, all that kind of stuff! *La-da-da-da-dum, da-dum, da-dum . . .*"

I felt a bit like a Martian. I didn't know any of the singers they were talking about. Given the state they were in, they'd be all night before they ran out of stock!

In the end, I opened another beer. I was starting to like it!

"How about Renaud?" Dédé said.

"Renaud! I'd forgotten all about him! Shit, I really liked him."

"At least he's on our side. He sings about the street."

"Do you remember 'The Mistral blows'?"

"How does it go?"

And Rico started singing, softly, in a weak, broken voice:

Sitting down here on this bench
Spending five minutes with you
Watching the sun going down
Recalling the good times we knew
They're gone, but I don't give a damn
We were the good guys, me and you . . .

I looked at Rico. Tears were welling up in his eyes.
Tears of drunkenness.
Tears of love.
"*And the mistral blows,*" Dédé shouted.
Rico took a long swig of whisky, put his arm around my shoulders, then sang, even more softly:

Love life, what more can I say
Though time sweeps everything away
And the laughter of children goes,
And the mistral blows
And the mistral blows

There was silence.
Dédé lit a cigarette. "Shit, Rico, you're going to make us cry."
Rico ignored him. He put his dirty index finger on my nose, and, looking me straight in the eyes, repeated:

. . . and the mistral blows . . .

He closed his eyes. I felt a knot in my stomach. Rico was leaving. He was going farther and farther away. From me, from us. From himself. And I couldn't stop him. Every word echoed in my head like a word of farewell.
It was the first night I'd spent in his crash pad. I'd have

preferred us to be alone. Dédé's presence was like a weight on us.

Like a weight on Rico.

Like death, I thought. That's exactly what I thought. How strange things are sometimes.

At that moment, Dédé started rummaging in his bag.

"By the way, I forgot to show you this."

He handed Rico a press cutting. A cruel smile hovered on his lips.

"What is it?"

"I cut it out of *Ouest-France*."

I went behind Rico and read the cutting over his shoulder.

"Rennes: Woman Raped and Killed in Her Own Home," the headline said. It dated from five weeks earlier.

Rico started shaking.

The woman was his wife.

Sophie.

She had been attacked when she came home from her daily jog in Thabor Park, between noon and 2 P.M. Her naked body had been found by her husband in the living room of their house on Rue de Fougeres. That was what the journalist reported.

Rico read the article a second time, more slowly. As if to convince himself that what he was reading had really happened.

According to the police, the journalist went on, the prime suspect was the victim's former husband, currently "of no fixed abode." According to friends, he had come to Rennes several times and had threatened her right outside her son's school. Several witnesses claimed to have seen him prowling around the house recently.

He was described as "an extremely jealous man, and a violent alcoholic."

Rico dropped the cutting. He looked at Dédé.

"She was a bitch, wasn't she? That's what you always said."

Rico punched him full in the face. On the nose. With a speed and strength that took us by surprise.

"Shit, man! You're crazy!"

Dédé's nose started gushing blood. His shirt was soon covered in it.

"Asshole! See what you did?"

Rico jumped on him, but he had exhausted all his energy, all his violence, in that single punch. He collapsed onto Dédé, weeping.

"And what about my son? Eh? Did you think about my son? He already lost his father. Now he's lost his mother."

Dédé shoved Rico away. They rolled on the mattress.

"Julien," Rico started sobbing.

There was an old pickax handle against the wall, and I grabbed it. If that bastard touched Rico, I'd murder him.

"You big crybaby," Dédé said, wiping his nose with a dirty cloth. "You wanted to strangle the bitch, didn't you? You were always saying that. But you never had the guts. You never had the guts to do anything in your life. That's why she dumped you."

"Get out," was all Rico said.

Dédé stood up.

So did I.

The pickax handle in my hand. Ready to strike.

We looked at each other.

Hate against hate.

If he'd been capable of something as bad as that, I told myself, he could easily have slept with Anne, the wife of Félix's boss. It might not have been true, but it suited me to think it was. And if it was true, it must have sickened Félix. Because he liked Anne. That was why he'd left.

Far from Dédé.

Far from everyone.

I kept telling myself that, as I gripped the pickax handle.

I took a step toward Dédé. "Get out of here, we said."

He picked up his bag. At the door, he turned and said to Rico, "I'm not sorry I did it . . ."

"Get out of here," I cried, raising the pickax handle.

"She was the best piece of ass I ever had."

And his laughter echoed along the gallery.

Rico was prostrate.

I went to him. "It's all right, Rico. He's gone. We can sleep now, if you want."

I handed him the bottle of whisky, and he took a good swig.

"It's all right, Rico."

"I need a smoke . . ."

I lit a cigarette, and put it in his mouth. He was shaking.

"What's Julien going to do? He's all alone."

"He isn't all alone."

The sadness in his eyes terrified me.

"I can't even go see him anymore."

"He isn't alone . . ."

He looked at me again. I lowered my head. I couldn't stand the despair deep in his eyes. Rico was crumbling inside. He would soon be nothing but dust. A heap of dust.

I took the plunge. "There's that guy who lived with her. Alain. He'll take care of Julien. He isn't his father, he isn't you, but he loves him, doesn't he? Don't you think so?"

Rico's raised his trembling hand to his mouth and dragged on his cigarette. The ash fell on his black parka.

"Rico?"

"Yeah."

"She went to live with the guy, didn't she? Because she loved him. And loving someone means trusting them, right?"

He stubbed out his cigarette, lay down on the mattress, and closed his eyes.

"Rico? Are you listening?"

He moved his head slightly.

"She trusted him, Rico." I lay down next to him, and whispered in his ear, "Trust him too. Julien isn't alone."

Then I picked up the teddy bear, and put it in Rico's arms. He hugged it.

My eyes were closing.

Some time during the night, Rico turned to me. I felt his hand stroking my hair, gently. Like my father used to.

"I love you, boy," he murmured.

It was like a dream, those words, that hand on my hair. I was dreaming, I told myself. Because it had to be a dream, those words, that hand in my hair.

"Daddy," I murmured.

I should have guessed it wasn't a dream.

I should have known that, when Rico's lips came to rest on my forehead and I felt his foul, damp breath on my face.

I should have woken up, instead of hugging the teddy bear.

I thought it was a dream.

We always think dreams are more beautiful than real life.

25.

ONE LAST SONG, AND WAITING, WAITING . . .

I jumped.
A noise. Like a heavy door closing. Then silence. A heavy silence. A damp silence. And that strong, greasy stench rising from the ground.

I opened my eyes in the darkness.

Two red eyes were staring at me.

The rat.

I leaped to my feet. Hugging the teddy bear to me.

"Rico!"

The rat didn't move. Neither did Rico.

"Rico!"

My hand groped for his back, his shoulder. To shake him. Wake him. Ask him to chase away the rat. I didn't dare move. Fear.

Rico.

Rico wasn't there anymore.

The door closing again.

I held the teddy bear even tighter.

"Don't be afraid, Zineb. It's only a rat."

I made a gesture in the darkness. A gesture of the hand. The rat didn't move. I had the impression his red eyes were getting bigger. The rat was becoming enormous. A wolf rat. A lion rat. An elephant rat.

"It'll be all right, Zineb! It'll be all right."

I thought of Tom and Jerry.

And I was Tom.

"Boo!" I yelled.

The rat still didn't move.

"Rico, please!"

Rico.

Rico wasn't there anymore.

That was when I pulled myself together. And it all made sense in my head. The way he'd stroked my hair. Kissed me on the forehead. Put the teddy bear in my arms.

He'd been saying goodbye.

"Rico!" I screamed. "No!"

I struck a match. The rat bolted toward the door and disappeared. I lit one of the candles. The flickering light played over the room.

The bike.

I threw aside the bags Rico had started piling up in front of the wheels. I pushed the bike as far as the door. I picked up a long piece of string that was lying on the floor and tied the teddy bear to my stomach.

"Let's go, Zineb. That O.K. with you?"

It was O.K. with him.

We couldn't leave Rico like that. Alone. No, we couldn't abandon him.

The end of the road. The lighthouse.

That's where he'll be, isn't it, Zineb?

The mistral had risen. It was cold. A gust of wind hit me in the face. The icy air lingered on my scars. They started smarting. I pulled my sweater up over my nose, and got on the bike.

"Are you ready, Zineb?"

I hurried along Rue François-Moisson, as far as Place de la Joliette. There, I turned onto the boulevard, under the highway bridge, between the wharves and the docks.

Pressing down on the pedals.

That damned bike may not have moved fast, but it moved. For every three times I pressed down on the pedals, the wheel turned once. And if there was a gust of wind, I'd have to press down another three times. The derailleur was squeaking, but I was making progress.

I had to go at least half a mile before I saw the bridge over the harbour that led from the wharves to the sea wall. Once on the other side, all I had to do was go the same distance, but in the other direction.

As far as the lighthouse.

Don't think.

Just pedal.

Rico. Wait for me.

Wait.

Gate 4.

No security guard in sight. He must be having coffee. It was coffee time. I had no idea what time it was. But it had to be coffee time. Day was just breaking. The more I pedalled, the bluer the sky turned. And the colder.

The mistral was behind me now. I felt as if I had wings. Each time I pressed down on the pedal, the wheel turned three times.

Don't think, Abdou.

Keep pedaling.

The last stretch.

The yellow jersey at the end. The podium.

The lighthouse.

Rico. Wait.

Don't go like this.

I passed freighters. Ready to set sail for other places. Africa. Asia. America.

On the road again.

How were those other places? Were they any better?

The end of the sea wall. The end of the road.

I threw the bike to the ground. I climbed the lighthouse

steps four at a time until I got to the platform. The icy mistral hit me in the face.

Rico was there.

Sitting on the ground. His body propped against the white stone. His eyes open. Staring out to sea. To the islands. To the horizon.

The most beautiful thing I've ever seen.

The thing Rico wanted to see.

A wave broke at the foot of the lighthouse and rose straight up into the sky.

The sun was putting on a firework display.

For Rico.

"Rico!"

It was no use.

Rico was smiling. His eyes were open.

I didn't dare look at him anymore.

I sat down next to him, untied Zineb, and held it between my legs.

What now?

I rested my head against Rico's shoulder, closed my eyes, and softly sang the song my father used to sing when times were bad:

I try so hard to remember
But my youth has slipped away
I've worn down the soles of my shoes
And I'm tired at the end of the day
My troubles are so many
That I can't remember any
I can't even remember my home
My luck has all gone away

My tears started flowing. Gently.

"Don't cry, Zineb. Don't cry."

*

A boat's siren echoed across the harbor.

Now the sun was high in the sky.

A white sun. A cold sun.

A sun for the dying, I thought.

A sun for the dying.

I slipped my hand into Rico's. Entwining my fingers with his. And waited.

I waited, you see.

Because, I told myself, life couldn't go on like this.

It can't go on.

ABOUT THE AUTHOR

Jean-Claude Izzo was born in Marseilles, France, in 1945. He achieved astounding success with his Marseilles Trilogy (*Total Chaos*, *Chourmo*, *Solea*). In addition to the books in this trilogy, his two novels *The Lost Sailors* and *A Sun for the Dying* and one collection of short stories have also enjoyed great success with both critics and the public. Izzo died in 2000, at the age of fifty-five.